CUPCAKE DIARIES

Emma raining cats and dogs...and cupcakes!

by coco simon

Simon Spotlight

New York   London   Toronto   Sydney   New Delhi

Emma
raining
cats and
dogs... and
cupcakes!

SIMON SPOTLIGHT

An imprint of Simon & Schuster Children's Publishing Division

1230 Avenue of the Americas, New York, New York 10020

First Simon Spotlight paperback edition January 2016

Copyright © 2016 by Simon & Schuster, Inc.

All rights reserved, including the right of reproduction
in whole or in part in any form.

SIMON SPOTLIGHT and colophon are registered trademarks of
Simon & Schuster, Inc.

Text by Elizabeth Doyle Carey

Chapter header illustrations by Julie Robine

Designed by Laura Roode

For information about special discounts for bulk purchases, please contact
Simon & Schuster Special Sales at 1-866-506-1949
or business@simonandschuster.com.

Manufactured in the United States of America 1215 OFF

2 4 6 8 10 9 7 5 3 1

ISBN 978-1-4814-5524-4 (pbk)

ISBN 978-1-4814-5525-1 (hc)

ISBN 978-1-4814-5526-8 (eBook)

Library of Congress Catalog Card Number 2015954541

CHAPTER 1

Arf!

𝐼 am a major dog-lover, but the barking was even getting to me! Twenty happy dogs in all shapes and sizes were excited and running around the grassy yard, playing with balls and ropes and jumping in and out of a doggy play structure in the center of the action.

Mrs. Barnett, the petite, blond director of ARF (Animal Rescue Fund), laughed and called above the din, "Why don't you girls come back to my office so we can hear ourselves think?"

The Cupcakers and I all laughed in agreement, and we followed her out of the fenced-in play yard and back down the tiled hall.

We, the Cupcake Club—me (Emma Taylor) and my best friends and business partners, Alexis

Becker, Mia Vélaz-Cruz, and Katie Brown—were at our local pet shelter for a meeting about some cupcakes we would be baking for an event they were having. The four of us have a business baking cupcakes for special events for friends, family, and clients (who often become like friends and family). We've done everything from kids' parties to movie premieres, celebrity weddings to moms' book clubs. We are creative and our cupcakes are reasonably priced, and we deliver! Our motto is: Professional cupcakes with a homemade twist.

Today we'd been recommended to ARF by a boy from our school who volunteers there—Diego Diaz. Diego is always Instagramming things about pets that need homes, and events being held at the shelter. He's really into helping animals and has raised a lot of awareness about abandoned animals, as well as helping to raise money for ARF. Now, ARF is having an adopt-a-pet event next weekend at our local park, and Diego suggested they hand out cupcakes to entice passersby to stop and mingle with the cats and dogs they'll have on-site for adoption. Mrs. Barnett loved the idea, so she'd contacted us and asked us to come in for a tour and meeting.

We settled into her cramped office—Alexis on an extra chair, taking notes on her laptop, Mia and

Katie perched on a windowsill, and me leaning in the doorway—and chatted about what kind of turnout ARF could expect for the park event and what they hoped to gain from it.

Mrs. Barnett explained, "Usually, we bring four kittens, two cats, at least two or three puppies, and then two older dogs. We expect to have about seventy people stop by the table during our three hours in the park. So maybe let's order . . . five dozen cupcakes, since I don't think everyone will take one. How does that sound?"

Alexis was nodding as she jotted it all down. "Great. So it's next Saturday. And we'll meet you at eleven, in the park, right? It's easier than you having to transport the cupcakes if we bring them there first."

"Yes. Thanks," agreed Mrs. Barnett.

We exchanged cell numbers.

"We'll come up with a design proposal for you to approve before this weekend," Alexis said and continued to outline the terms, but all I could think about were the poor animals that needed homes. Cupcakes were far from my mind.

"Um, excuse me, Mrs. Barnett? How many of the animals do you usually place at an event like this?" I had to know.

Mrs. Barnett smiled. "The kittens are the easiest. We'll almost always place a kitten. About once every three or four months, we'll place a puppy. Maybe once a year we place an older dog this way. But we do yield about five on-site visits from these events. . . ."

I must have looked confused, because she looked at me kindly and explained.

"People follow up with a visit here to the shelter. And those tend to be more productive for us than the park events because, of course, if people are bothering to come see us, they are usually pretty ready to adopt."

I felt my chest relax a little. "Oh. Good. I just can't stand to think of all those poor animals . . ." I wasn't sure how to finish my sentence.

Mrs. Barnett nodded sympathetically. "I know. We are a no-kill shelter, though. We won't put down animals just because we can't find homes for them. Every once in a while there's a really difficult animal that we have to refer elsewhere—severe biters, feral cats, attack dogs, what have you—but we do eventually find someplace for everyone. It can sometimes take more than a year."

"Poor little guys," I said.

She nodded again, then she said briskly, "But

our pity really doesn't help them. People need to have their animals spayed and neutered so they don't reproduce, and we need to keep the profile of ARF in the public eye so people continue to donate to us. That's where your cupcakes come in!" She stood up to signal that our meeting was over.

Alexis closed her laptop and stood to shake Mrs. Barnett's hand. "Thanks so much for the opportunity to bake for you," said Alexis. "We're sure you'll love the results!"

Mrs. Barnett laughed and patted her stomach. "That's what I'm worried about!"

We laughed with her, and my stress eased a bit. Alexis was always so professional, and it kept things flowing. We were quickly outside and ready to call for our ride. Even from the sidewalk, though, the barking was pretty crazy.

"Those poor doggies," I said.

Katie looped her arm across my shoulders and gave me a squeeze. "I know. I could tell you were taking it hard, you little animal lover, you."

"I'm going to give Tiki and Milkshake extra doggy treats when I get home today," said Mia. She shook her head as if to clear her mind. "It's so sad that people just ditch their pets like that. I can't even imagine it. It just breaks my heart."

"Pets are expensive," Alexis said briskly. "It would be sadder if they ditched their kids when times got tough."

"Alexis!" I reprimanded her.

She shrugged. "Sorry, but it's true. I'm stunned by how much money is spent on pets in this country."

"All right, boss lady! We don't need an economics lesson!" teased Mia.

Alexis sniffed. "I might just have to go into the pet-supply business when I get older."

We giggled, and pretty soon after, my dad rolled up in our minivan and we piled in.

"How did it go?" he asked as the door slid shut behind us.

"Oh, Dad, it was so sad!" I wailed, buckling my seat belt. "There are so many animals that need homes!"

He nodded. "I can't even go into those places. I'd come out with enough pets to fill an ark!"

"Maybe we should!" I said enthusiastically.

But he smiled and shook his head. "I don't deny that we are getting closer to convincing your mom to get a dog. *But there is still much work for us to do . . . ,*" he said in a fake formal tone.

6

My three brothers and I have wanted a dog for years, ever since our old Lab, Sissy, died. My youngest brother, Jake, in particular, is dying for a dog of his own. Since he's pretty spoiled, he'll probably get it. I'm just hoping he'll be willing to share.

I've always loved dogs—I like cats, too, but not in the same way—and snuggling with Sissy is one of my earliest memories. Her warm, soft fur; her silky ears that she'd let me play with whenever I wanted; her strong, quiet heartbeat when I laid my head on her and used her as a TV pillow; that coziness that always made me feel happy. I loved how safe she made me feel and how she was always overjoyed to see me. It was the best feeling.

For the past few years I've been earning extra money by walking dogs in the neighborhood. I used to have a bigger business, but it got overwhelming and I had to dial it back. It is pretty incredible how many pets are out there and how much money can be made from them. But as much as I love other people's pets, there's nothing quite like having one of your own. More importantly, I just don't like to see animals suffer.

"It's just so sad, all those animals in there—"

Alexis interrupted me. "Wait. It would be sad if they were all boxed in, in cages and whatever. But it's *not* sad, because ARF has those play yards for the dogs, and that indoor playroom for the cats, and all the volunteers, and good food. . . . It's pricey but worth it. Kind of like a boarding school for pets. Think of it that way!" Then she frowned. "Hmm. Maybe that's an idea for my Future Business Leaders project." She whipped out her phone and began making notes, her fingers flying.

I laughed and shook my head. Alexis is so practical and driven.

"Listen, what are we thinking to bake for them?" asked Katie. "I have loads of cute ideas on my computer that could be good. We could do little sugar cookies cut in the shape of dog bones on top of chocolate frosting. . . ."

"Cute," agreed Mia. "Or paw prints?"

Katie nodded. "Or I have some more elaborate designs we could try. . . ."

I agreed. "I'm up for anything. I think Mrs. Barnett is too. Lex?"

"Hmmm?" She was texting away madly.

"I had a thought. . . ."

Mia and Katie looked at me as we turned onto Katie's street.

"Lex?" I asked again quietly.

She looked up at me.

"What if we didn't charge?"

Alexis blinked, not comprehending. "What?" she said finally.

I glanced at the other two Cupcakers. They understood what I was getting at. Mia's eyebrows were raised in surprise, but a smile was forming on Katie's face.

"What if we made the cupcakes a donation?" I pressed.

Alexis sighed a huge sigh. I could see her running the numbers in her head. . . . Well, sixty cupcakes . . . and at a unit cost of seventy-five cents per . . . plus transport time . . .

"Just think about it, okay?" I asked.

Mia and Katie nodded from the back row.

"Okay. I'll think about it. I just don't want to set a bad precedent. Lots of our clients are nonprofits," said Alexis.

"I know. But those poor doggies. . . ."

"We've never done that before," continued Alexis. "Not charged."

"What about a deep discount?" offered Mia.

Alexis started to nod.

"Don't decide now, Lex. You look into it, and we'll discuss it at the weekly meeting on Wednesday, okay?" I felt good, though. I could tell

I was going to win this one. I smiled to myself.

"By the way," added Katie, "we should do something as a thank-you to Diego Diaz for the referral, don't you think?"

"Good call!" I agreed heartily. A smile spread across my face, and I could feel a blush coming on. Katie looked at me, and I am sure she noticed my reaction to hearing Diego's name, but she was kind enough to not say anything.

"Yeah. Maybe let's bake a few extra for him, and Emma can drop them off," Mia teased. So now I was really blushing. I gestured to my dad driving, and they got my drift and quieted down quickly, thank goodness.

We pulled into Katie's driveway, which was a welcome distraction from the topic at hand.

"Okay, Katie! Hope to see you soon!" joked my dad. My friends come over all the time.

"Thanks, Mr. Taylor," she said, sliding open the door and hopping out onto the blacktop.

"So four o'clock at the movies?" she asked.

We agreed. We'd meet after we finished our weekend homework, and then we'd see the new Liam Carey movie and have a quick bite at the mall.

Our next stop was Mia's, and of course, what I was dreading most happened. Her cousin Sebastian, who I thought was really cute when he moved here a while ago, was hanging out with her step-brother, Dan, on the front stoop. I'd had a crush on Sebastian, but things got all mixed up and he asked out Katie, and now I just really never want to see him again. Even if he is still pretty cute.

Mia saw them and glanced quickly at me. "Thanks, Mr. Taylor. I can get out right here. . . ." We were still a house away, and my dad was obviously aiming to pull into her driveway. Then there'd be no avoiding Sebastian.

"Oh, it's no problem," said my dad.

"Dad," I said sharply. "Please don't pull in." I sank low in my seat in hopes the boys wouldn't see me through the tinted window.

He gave me a weird look in the rearview mirror, but luckily, he did as we asked. Mia slid open the door on the street side so she wouldn't have to climb over me.

"Careful, honey!" said my dad as a car inched by on that side.

I squeezed Mia's hand before she left. She knew I was thanking her for her consideration in not exposing me to Sebastian again. She squeezed back.

"Thanks, Mr. Taylor. See you girls at the mall!"

She hopped out and pushed the close button on the door so fast, it nearly caught her as she exited. "Oops!" She laughed.

My dad was shaking his head. "You girls are going to be the death of me," he said. "Always some kind of mystery agenda going on. . . ." He eased his way back onto the road and continued until we dropped off Alexis.

As we drove home from her house, I could feel my dad checking on me in the rearview mirror again. "Everything okay, lovebug?" he asked.

I nodded and looked out the window. The Sebastian and Katie thing had been embarrassing, and I was only just feeling like I was over it, but now it was all back again. I was new to the whole boy thing, and I wasn't sure I liked this kind of drama.

"Who's Diego?" Dad asked with a smile.

Oh, well, Diego was another story. Not much of a story, actually. Yet. Maybe. A smiled bloomed on my face, anyway. "A guy from school."

My dad smiled again at me, clearly waiting for more. But I just continued to look out the window. There truly *wasn't* any more to say right now. So after a pause, during which my dad realized he wasn't getting any info out of me, he reached over and turned up the radio, which was playing some dorky eighties song from his youth. Then he bopped his head and patted the steering wheel in time to the beat for the final part of our trip home. It was majorly embarrassing.

CHAPTER 2

Rocky

At the kitchen table during our Sunday night dinner, the topic turned to birthdays, including Jake's, which was coming up.

Jake wanted to have a circus-style birthday at home, complete with carnival games like knock-down-the-bottles; beanbag toss; and throw a Ping-Pong, win a goldfish. He also wanted a clown to come for entertainment.

"Wow. Sounds elaborate," I said. Was there any way my parents would go for this?

"It might just be easier to take Jake and a couple of friends to the circus," suggested my dad.

"Yes!" cried Jake. "The Big Apple Circus! With all the dogs doing tricks! Oh, please! Can we? I heard about it in school!"

My mom gave my dad a we-should-have-discussed-this-first glare, and then she said, "Let me look it up online, honey. They travel, so they're only around at certain times of the year, okay?"

Jake seemed okay with that, but he continued to talk about the dogs. He said they'd read a great book in school called *Stay*, which was about trained circus dogs and their owner, and if Jake and his friends could go to the circus for his birthday, he wanted the book to be the party favor.

"We'll see, Jake," said my dad. "Meanwhile, speaking of dogs . . ."

My dad proceeded to tell us that Jake's soccer coach was asking around for a family to dogsit for his dog, Rocky, in a couple of weeks. Coach Mike and his wife, who were newlyweds, were going to be moving soon, and they needed to go house-hunting out of town. They couldn't take their dog on the three-day trip.

"Rocky is soooo awesome, Mom!" said Jake, spearing a bite of meatball on his fork. "He chases down every soccer ball, and he runs with us, and he is just. So. Cool." He popped the meatball into his mouth and chewed thoughtfully. Then he swallowed and said, "When I get a dog, I want one just like Rocky."

My mom said, "Hmm. What kind of a dog is he?"

"Um, he's brownish? Reddish? With curly hair?" said Jake.

"That's not a breed, dude." My oldest brother, Sam, laughed.

Jake shrugged. "He's fluffy. He's a fluff dog."

"He's a goldendoodle, I think," said my dad. "Half poodle, half golden retriever."

"Must be a pretty big dog," said my mom.

My dad shrugged. "Not as big as you would think. It's kind of medium-size, copper colored. He's a sweet dog."

"Is he a puppy?" asked my mom.

"Puppyish. Maybe a year and a half or so?" said my dad, squinting as he tried to recall.

"Maybe we *should* dogsit him!" I said, looking around the table.

"Major hassle," said Matt, my brother who is a year older than I am. He shook his head.

But Jake agreed with me. "Yeah! Let's! That would be awesome!" he said, beaming. "Rocky loves me! He could sleep on my bed with me, and I could feed him and walk him, and we could play outside. . . ."

My dad wiped his mouth with his napkin and

pushed his chair back a bit. He took a long sip of his water and cleared his throat. We all looked at him expectantly.

"It's a lot of work," he began.

"It would be a good test drive to see if we want to get a new dog!" I said.

"Yeah! Then I could get one for my birthday!" agreed Jake.

My mom laughed. "Not so fast, partner. Like dad said, dogs *are* a lot of work. I'm still enjoying all the free time I've had since Sissy . . ."

"Mom! That's so mean! You're glad Sissy died?" I cried.

Sam laughed. "You are a bad mom!" he teased.

My mom smiled. "No, of course I miss our little Sissy, with all my heart. But the time she took up . . . and the expense . . ."

"I could take care of a dog," Jake said, sitting up straight in his chair. "I'm responsible."

Matt laughed and milk spurted out of his nose.

"Gross!" I cried, covering my eyes.

"Okay, calm down, everyone. Your mom and I will discuss dogsitting for Rocky. We'll let you know later in the week, okay?"

I shrugged. I didn't really care one way or another about the dogsitting. I just wanted them to say we could get our own dog. But Jake, I think, misread the whole thing.

"Yesss!" he cried, pumping his fists in the air. "We're getting a dog! Rocky's coming to live with us!"

"Oh, brother. Good luck," Sam said, excusing himself to help clear the table.

My mom rolled her eyes. "Here we go," she said. Jake tends to be a little spoiled, and when he gets something in his head . . . well, he usually ends up getting his way.

Walking home from school on Monday, Katie was showing us photos of pet cupcakes on her phone.

"And look at these! Aren't these adorable?" She flashed a pic of cupcakes that had been topped with shaggy white dogs' heads, with tiny chocolate candy circles for the eyes and noses.

"Ooh!" we squealed. They were adorable. "Let's do those! Would it be hard?" I asked.

"How much do you think they would cost to make?" asked Alexis.

Katie made the photo bigger so we could see more details. "The top of the cupcake is really high, so they must add a little something extra on top— like a doughnut hole—that they frost. So there's the cake ingredients and liners, we'll need extra frosting, and the doughnut holes or whatever, and then the little candies. Not too expensive, actually."

"Just a lot of labor, it looks like," Alexis said approvingly. She didn't mind hard work; it was expensive cupcake decorations she liked to avoid when possible.

"We can call them *pupcakes!*" said Mia, who is always so creative.

"Love!" I said emphatically.

"I also found these," Katie said, opening another photo and showing it around. They were cat cupcakes, with colored M&Ms for eyes, set on their edges, and chocolate gel-frosting whiskers coming out of a chocolate chip nose. They were very cute too.

"I like these even better!" said Mia. "High impact and less work. *Catcakes!*"

Alexis took the phone and studied the picture. "Also reasonably priced components. Good work, Katie!"

Katie beamed.

"I'll run the pricing and then see what kind of discount we can afford to give them," offered Alexis.

"Thanks!" I said. Even if we didn't end up flat

out donating the cupcakes, it would still be nice to offer a big discount to ARF. I was glad Alexis was coming around.

"Ooooh, don't look now, Em, but Diego Diaz is coming this way!" Mia whispered. I looked up quickly, and there was Diego, walking right toward us. I was trying to think of something to say, but Katie beat me to the punch.

"Hey, Diego!" said Katie.

I looked directly at him, and there he was, smiling at me. "Hey!" I said, wiggling my fingers in a little wave. I was grinning from ear to ear.

"I heard you guys are going to bake cupcakes for the ARF event on Saturday," he said. "That's awesome! I'd better get there early so I get one!"

"Oh, no rush. We're making you some of your own," said Katie.

"Katie!" Alexis scolded, but with a smile. "You guys are giving away all our profits!"

"Alexis! That's so rude!" I blurted. I couldn't help myself.

Diego laughed and put his hands out, as if refusing. "Don't give me any. I'm happy to get one at the event."

"No, I'm sorry. Emma's right," Alexis said, smacking her forehead. "We're giving you some cupcakes as a commission, for getting us the job. I forgot for a minute."

"Well, in that case, how can I say no?" Diego laughed. He had a great smile, with strong, white, even teeth that shined against his caramel-colored skin.

"Thank you for referring us," I said politely, staring daggers at Alexis.

"Oh, no problem. It seemed like a good fit. And I know it will draw people to our table. I've seen you Cupcake girls in action. No one can say no to a cupcake."

"It's pretty hard to say no to puppies and kittens too, right?" I added. I was trying hard to keep the conversation going. Diego was so nice, and I always felt happy when I was around him.

"You'd be surprised," he said. "It's pretty tough to get homes for those little guys."

"It's so sad," I agreed.

He shrugged. "That's why I like volunteering at ARF. It's not as sad when you feel like you're helping."

I didn't want to tell him that I pored over all his posts on Instagram and that I really admired what he was doing to raise awareness on this topic.

"Well, we'll have some cupcakes for you on

Saturday, and that will be cheerful," I said with a big smile, to change the subject.

"Great. Thanks. I'm looking forward to it. Catch you later!" he said.

Mia waited until he was out of earshot and then turned to me and nodded. "He totally likes you," Mia said knowledgably.

"And you were cool as a cucumber," Alexis said, shaking her head. "It's all that practice hanging out with cute boys at home." Alexis is in love with Matt, which is sometimes fun and convenient and sometimes a total drag, depending on my mood.

"I don't *have* any cute boys in my house," I joked. "Hey, speaking of which . . ." I explained about Jake, and how we might get a dog, and how we might dogsit first.

Mia shook her head with a laugh. "I don't know if dogsitting is the way to go if you want to get a dog. It could go so wrong that your parents decide against it for good!"

"Oh, that's true. I hadn't thought of that," I said. I frowned; I had been thinking dogsitting would do the opposite.

"But hey, I have an idea! Maybe Jake would like to come look after Tiki and Milkshake for me this Saturday, while I'm at my dad's? I mean, my mom and Eddie are here, but maybe he'd walk them and play with them a little? I worry that they get so lonely when I'm not there, since no one looks after them the way that I do. I'll pay him!"

"Thanks. You don't need to pay him," I protested. "As if you don't do enough for that kid already! I'm sure he'll want to."

We agreed that she should ask Jake when we had our Cupcake meeting at my house on Wednesday.

"YES!!!" Jake said, pumping his fist in the air. It was Wednesday after school, and Jake made it clear that he wanted to dogsit Tiki and Milkshake.

Mia laughed. "Okay! I like the enthusiasm!"

"And you know why this is a good idea?" asked Jake. "Because we are getting a dog named Rocky soon, and this way I can practice so I'll be ready."

Oh dear. "Um, Jake?" I said gently. "We're not getting Rocky. We just might dogsit him for three days. And if that goes well, then, maybe maybe maybe, Mom and Dad will let us get our own dog. Remember?"

"Right. Named Rocky," he agreed.

Whatever.

"Mia, do you want to just write out a little schedule for Jake so he knows what you need?"

Over Jake's head, I mouthed, *Not too much*. Mia got my drift and nodded back at me.

"That's a great idea," said Mia. "Jake, I'm putting this on the list. Please come over and walk Tiki and Milkshake at ten o'clock on Saturday, okay? Their leashes hang on a hook right inside the front door. How about twice around the block? They'll need to do their bathroom business. And when you bring them back in, would you give them each a treat from the jar on the front hall table, please?"

"Yup. Uh-huh. I can do that. No prob." Jake drew himself up to his full height. Maybe this would be a good learning experience for him, I thought. We'd just have to work out who was going to bring him over. It obviously couldn't be me, because I did not want to run into Sebastian while I was there. Also, it might be kind of strange to be at Mia's without her. I'd let my parents work it out. It wasn't my problem.

Mia wrote it all out and left the sheet on the kitchen counter. I'd make sure my mom saw it when she got home from work.

Meanwhile, our sample cupcakes had come out of the oven and cooled for long enough; it was time to frost them.

24

"Okay, Jake. Time for homework. We'll call you when it's time to taste the cupcakes. Run along now." I scooted him out of the kitchen.

Jake headed up to his room, and I turned my attention to our cupcake supplies. I poured some of the little chocolate circles into a dish, as well as some M&Ms in another little dish, and some mini chocolate chips. Then I snipped off the top from a chocolate gel-frosting tube and set that out, too, all neatly aligned.

I checked on everyone else's progress. Katie had made a big batch of light, fluffy, white frosting. Mia was cutting doughnut holes in half on a cutting board, and Alexis was on her calculator, figuring out the unit cost of each of the cupcakes. I love when we're in a groove and working hard on a new recipe or design. We're like a well-oiled machine. It makes me so happy.

"So?" I asked, peering over Lex's shoulder at her laptop.

"Hmm," she said. Then she looked up. "I guess we could charge them half price. The only thing I worry about is if it goes really well and they want to reorder on another weekend, and then we're stuck with this low pricing."

She had a point. And what if they became

good clients? Regular clients? Like Mona at The Special Day bridal salon and who we deliver to every week.

Luckily, Mia piped up. "Just offer them at half price and say it's an introductory discount and we hope the cupcakes add a lot of value to their event."

Alexis nodded. She loves business terminology. "Introductory discount is the way to go. Good call, Mia."

"So half price?" I asked.

"Yup," agreed Alexis.

"Thanks!" I said and squeezed her in a half-hug, since she really doesn't like hugs. "You're the best CEO ever! Those poor animals are lucky to have you as their friend."

She patted my hand briskly and slid out from under my arm. "Let's see how these turn out, first."

Mia and Katie assembled a few of the doughnut hole–and–cupcake combos, and then Mia began piping the frosting over them, referring to the photos I'd pulled up on my laptop. I helped frost and assemble the cat cupcakes, and soon we had completed about six each of the pupcakes and catcakes. They looked fantastic!

"Wow, you guys!" Mia said. "These are some of our cutest cupcakes ever!"

Katie was snapping pics with her phone to upload on to our website. "I agree. They came out just as well as the ones in the photos I found online!"

"Wait till Diego sees them!" I blurted.

"We have to remember to bake the extra cakes for him too, Alexis," said Katie.

"Uhhhhn." Alexis sighed heavily, and made a note on her laptop, but she didn't complain further.

"Whatever happened with your crush on Sebastian?" asked Mia, sidling up to me as the other girls discussed which platters we should use for display.

I shrugged. "I don't know, I think I was interested just because he was new and different. I'm over him." It wasn't totally true because if I saw him (like the other day in the van), I would definitely get all shaky. Seeing him was to be avoided. But also, Diego was a nice distraction, and now he'd popped back up again. So yes, I was technically over Sebastian.

"Good," said Mia. "I just don't want things to continue to be awkward. Especially when you have to come to my house."

I panicked. "Oh, I'm not coming to your *house*! Not if Sebastian's going to be there!"

Mia smacked her forehead. "That's what I'm talking about. So you're not over him!"

"Let's just take it day by day," I said. *"Día a día."*

Katie and Alexis came back from the pantry. "Hey, Em? Why don't we just give these samples to Diego?" suggested Alexis. "What else would we do with them, anyway?"

Just then Jake walked in from the front hall, and Matt came in the back door, both right on cue. "Cupcakes!" they cried in unison.

We laughed. It was perfect timing, like on a TV show.

"Okay, all but two," Alexis said, softening at the sight of Matt.

"I can have all but two?" he said happily.

"No!" we all shouted.

Alexis clarified. "Someone else gets all but two. You two get the two. Get it?"

"Okay, take it easy, bossy pants!"

I boxed up all but two cupcakes and wrote Diego's name on a piece of masking tape on the box. "Matt, will you please take these to Diego Diaz tomorrow at school?"

"Uh-uhn." He shook his head, because his mouth was full of cupcake. I'd known he would say that.

"You do it, Emma!" Katie said with a smile and a meaningful look.

I felt a blush start to rise, and I didn't want Matt to see it. "Fine," I said, ducking my head. "Fine."

CHAPTER 3

Treats!

$\mathcal{I}$ got to school early with my cupcake box and wandered the halls, looking for Diego's locker and feeling like a nerd. Was I really going to hand him this thing? It wouldn't fit in his locker. He'd have to stash them in his homeroom, and then everyone will be begging cupcakes from him all day. We should have just waited and made extra cupcakes for him on Saturday. Oh, why did I let Alexis pawn our samples like this, just to save money?! I was so nervous and frustrated.

After doing a few laps of the areas where I thought his locker might be, I was getting ready to give up and stash the cupcakes in *my* homeroom, and then I spied him.

"Diego!" I called, blushing from saying his name.

He turned, and his face broke into a wide grin. He was so cute!

I waved my usual little wave and walked to meet him halfway.

"Hi!" he said.

"Hi! I have your commission here. Sorry. I just realized it's kind of bulky. I hope it's not a hassle."

"Are you kidding?" His eyes lit up. "This is awesome. You guys didn't need to do this. But I am so glad you did!" His brown eyes sparkled, and his whole face crinkled up when he smiled.

I shrugged awkwardly. "Well, we really appreciate you referring us. And for such a good cause. Thanks." I wanted to keep chatting, but I also didn't want to keep him too long, in case there was somewhere he needed to be.

"Thanks so much," he said.

We both stood there for a minute, looking around nervously and smiling.

"Well, I should be . . ."

"Anyway . . ."

We'd both spoken at the same time, and we laughed.

"Thanks, Emma. I've got to run. I will really enjoy these." He took a peek at the cupcakes. "Oh! Dogs and cats, I get it. Funny! Thanks again.

Maybe they'll even let me have one at the event on Saturday. Will you be there?" he asked.

I nodded. "Yup."

"Great. So if I don't see you before then, till Saturday." He gave me a funny salute, smiled at me, and then walked off.

"Bye," I said, smiling, and I kept smiling even after he had walked away. Then I spun on my heel and hurried up to class.

On Friday, we went to Alexis's to bake. Mia had left for her dad's, so it was just the three of us. We had our standing order of mini white-on-white cupcakes for Mona, at The Special Day. We could make those with our eyes closed. Then we had the five dozen cupcakes for the ARF event, which was a little more time-consuming with only the three of us working.

"So what time do we need to be at the park for this?" I asked, looking at my watch. It was getting late—close to six—and I wondered if maybe we should finish up in the morning.

"Eleven o'clock," said Alexis.

"That's not too bad," I said.

"It's too bad Mia's not here," said Katie. "I miss her skills!"

32

"I know," agreed Alexis. Her tongue poked out between her teeth, and she carefully piped white "dog fur" onto yet another cupcake.

"So we'll meet here at around ten thirty?" I asked.

Alexis nodded. "My dad will drive us over. I'll take Mona's minis, too."

"I can't wait to see all the animals tomorrow morning," said Katie.

"Wait! Animals . . . tomorrow morning! Jake's supposed to be taking care of Tiki and Milkshake tomorrow at ten, and I forgot to give my mom that sheet Mia wrote down!" I panicked. Quickly, I texted my parents to see who could take Jake over there.

I tapped my fingers impatiently while I waited for a reply.

My phone chirped, and I looked down. Sorry, love. Have to work half day. Ask Dad, texted my mom.

At the exact same time, a reply came in from my dad. Driving Matt's crew to a game an hour away. Leaving at 8. Ask Mom. Love, Dad.

"Noooo!" I wailed and collapsed on the counter.

"Bad news?" Alexis asked ironically.

I stood up straight. "I volunteered Jake to take care of Mia's dogs and now I have to get him over there by ten and have him walk the dogs around the block twice." The worst part was not only that I'd be late for the ARF event (and Diego!), but that I might have to see Sebastian, since he was always over there, hanging with Mia's stepbrother. But I didn't want to get into that.

"We'll be fine, just the two of us. You don't need to come to the ARF thing. It's okay," Katie said kindly.

"Well, but . . . I hate to leave you in a lurch. . . ." I began awkwardly.

"Oh, I know! It's Diego!" said Alexis, teasing me. "You don't even care about us. You are so busted. You just want to see Diego! Admit it!"

I laughed and blushed.

"Ooh! She's blushing!" exclaimed Katie, but she wasn't being mean, just funny.

"Okay, that *is* part of it," I said.

"Like ninety percent of it, I'd say," joked Alexis.

"Whatever. I'll be fast. I guess I'm stuck with Jake, anyway, for the morning, so we'll just meet you at the park after. I suppose this means we'd better finish up tonight, though."

We redoubled our efforts and finished by seven. Alexis's mom dropped me off, but not before I told them I'd see Alexis and Katie at the park at ten forty-five at the very latest the next morning.

I couldn't wait for the next day. I had everything planned out perfectly.

Boy, was I wrong.

Things started off okay, but Jake is always slow, no matter what. The good news was he was excited about seeing Mia's dogs, and he was proud to have a job to do, so that helped get us out the door. It was ten fifteen by the time we finally got into the car to Mia's, though (Sam agreed to drop us off on his way to the library), and as we approached the house, who did I spy on Mia's stoop but Sebastian and Dan.

"Whoa! Stop the car!" I said to Sam about three houses before Mia's.

"What?" Sam looked at me like I was crazy.

"I'm getting out here. Jake, get the leashes and the dogs, and I'll meet you on the corner, okay?"

Jake was even prouder, now that he was really on his own. "Okay!"

"Why are you getting out, weirdy?" Sam asked with a quizzical look on his face.

I snapped open the door. "I just am. Thanks for the ride. Bye."

"Okaaaaay. Whatevs! Bye," said Sam, and he

continued up the road and turned into Mia's driveway.

I turned on my heel and walked back to the corner to wait for Jake. I checked my phone: 10:28. Ugh. Like everything I did with Jake, this was going to take a lot longer than planned. I sighed heavily and tapped my foot.

Minutes went by. I checked my phone again: 10:33. Where *was* this kid? I craned my neck to see if I could see him. He was not coming, as far as I could tell.

I waited a few minutes more. Now, it was 10:38. It did not take ten minutes to snap two leashes on two collars and walk three-house lengths. "Come *on*, Jake!" I muttered out loud in frustration.

Ten forty.

I had to go get him. Thank goodness I'd taken extra time getting ready this morning, in anticipation of seeing Diego. I had blown my hair dry, put on cute earrings, and was wearing my best skinny jeans with my favorite striped T-shirt and a fitted, zip-up floral fleece over it, with cool flat sneakers. If I ended up seeing Sebastian, at least I'd look good.

When I reached the house before Mia's, I could see some chaos in Mia's front yard. Jake and Dan and Sebastian seemed to be chasing Tiki and Milkshake around. Everyone was kind of laughing, but they couldn't catch the dogs. Why were they outside not on their leashes?

"Jake? Come on! We have to go!" I yelled from the sidewalk. But he either didn't hear me or didn't care.

"I've got this one cornered!" Sebastian yelled from in front of a bush. "Bring the leash!"

He dived to scoop up Tiki, but Tiki darted away and all Sebastian scooped was air.

This was a disaster. All I could think about was how late I was going to be for our Cupcake event, and more important, that I might miss seeing Diego. My anger made me brave, and I stormed across the yard.

"What is going on here?" I yelled.

Dan and Sebastian turned to me, laughing, but Jake was stressed.

"Oh, Emmy! The dogs wouldn't follow me to meet you! I've been trying to catch them!"

I was confused. "But they should follow you when they're on their leashes, Jake," I said.

But he was shaking his head. "You didn't say to put on their leashes. You just said get the dogs, get their leashes. When I opened the door to have them follow me, they ran away."

Dan and Sebastian nodded. "It really wasn't his fault," said Dan. "It's just they're never let out in the front off–leash, so I think they're excited."

Sebastian nodded and added, "Plus, since he's a kid, they think he's playing with them."

I was mad, though. It feels like something always goes wrong when I'm watching Jake. I sighed heavily in frustration, then I remembered something. I stormed up the front stoop and past the front door. I grabbed two treats from the jar on the hall table and came back out.

"Treats!" I called. "Tiki! Milkshake! Treats!"

The two dogs came bounding over to me instantly.

"Sit!" I commanded. They sat.

"Wow!" said Sebastian. "Impressive."

"Stay!" I held my hand flat, palm side down. The dogs stayed. They were watching the treats in my other hand. It wasn't like they were doing it because I was so commanding, but whatever.

"Okay, Jake, clip the leashes on to the little rings on their collars, please."

Jake rushed over and did just that. The leashes were mismatched—I could tell by the colors of the collars and the leashes which went with which, but I wasn't going to get into dog fashion right now

38

and correct Jake. (But it would have bugged Mia!)

"Give the leashes a little tug to make sure they're secure, Jake. Okay." I dropped a treat before each dog, and they snatched them up and stayed sitting. "All right, Jake, let's go."

I stole a glance at Dan and Sebastian, and I could see they really were impressed by my dog handling. I couldn't help being a tiny bit proud. *Take that, Sebastian!* I thought.

"Bye!" they said in wonder as we trotted off down the yard.

"We'll be back in a little bit," I said, waving without turning around.

Jake was still a little miffed, I could see, but my irritation with him had settled down. He was right. I hadn't said the dogs needed to be on their leashes before he let them out. Sometimes I forget how young he is and how much still needs to be explained to him. I tried to think of something to soothe his ruffled pride.

"Jake, good job with the dogs back there. You got them all warmed up for their walk. It won't take long for them to do their business now. Plus, I don't think anyone plays with them that much, like you did back there. They were psyched."

Jake gave a sigh of relief. "You think? Yeah. I

guess you're right. They were having a lot of fun with me." He smiled, thinking of it.

And I was right. Tiki and Milkshake were extremely efficient. They did what they needed to do very quickly, and then we walked them briskly around the block twice, anyway, just for exercise. Jake refused to pick up their messes in the little doggy poop bags, so I did it. I didn't want to have to fight him, even if it really was his job.

Back at Mia's, I was relieved to see that Dan and Sebastian were gone. Inside, we gave each of the dogs another little treat, hung up their leashes, and watched them dash right to their doggy beds for a well-earned nap.

"Good job, Jake," I said. "Now let's go to the park for the ARF event."

I breathed a sigh of relief and then looked at my phone. Gulp. It was eleven thirty. Quickly, I texted Katie and Alexis that I was on my way, and Jake and I rushed over, taking a bus for part of the way.

I was out of breath by the time we got there at noon, an hour late—really, an hour and a half if you count the set-up time that I missed. But it was a beautiful day, and there were lots of people walking around and playing in the park. Jake and I found the ARF truck, and I was happy to see it was pretty busy.

"Come on, Jake!" I called, and we ran the last little bit of the way, laughing the whole time.

It was warm, so I peeled off my fleece, and I noticed most other people were in short sleeves—some even in shorts.

"Hey, girls!" I called to Katie and Alexis. They were standing a little off to the side. Not really working the table but available if needed.

"Hey!" they squealed, seeing me.

I looked around for Diego, trying not to give away what I was doing.

"He's not here," Alexis said, reading my mind, as usual.

"What? But he said he was coming for sure. That's so weird," I said.

Katie shrugged. "You never know. Maybe he'll still come."

Disappointed, I turned to survey the scene. "How's it going?" I asked.

"Lots of people are stopping. Most people leave with at least one cupcake . . . ," said Katie.

I peered into the playpens they'd set up for the animals. "Any takers?" I whispered, as if the animals could hear me and understand. Jake was actually inside the dog pen, laughing and letting the dogs lick him. It was pretty cute.

"Nope," said Alexis. "It's like what Mrs. Barnett said. The kittens get a lot of attention. A few people check out the dogs . . ."

"But no one has taken any of them home," finished Katie.

"Hmm," I said. "Well, maybe I'll go check in with Mrs. Barnett. . . . Can you guys keep an eye on Jake while I ask her?"

"You mean ask her where Diego is?" teased Alexis with a grin.

"Shh!" I said as I wandered away. But just as I rounded the truck to say hi, there he was!

"Diego!" I said happily. He was wearing a baseball hat pulled low, sunglasses, a turtleneck and sweatpants, despite the heat. Kind of a weird outfit for a warm fall day.

"Hey, what's up?" he asked, not his usual friendly self. He'd barely looked at me. It was like he was trying to get away.

"Um, are you just getting here?" I asked.

"Yup. You?" He looked elsewhere as he talked.

"Diego?" I tried to look at him directly, but he turned his face. "Everything okay?" I asked.

"Oh, what? Yeah. I just . . . need to check in with Mrs. Barnett. I'm . . . Let me just pop over there. See ya," he said.

"Okay. See ya," I said miserably. It was like we were never friends. What on Earth? I was mortified. And here I'd been expecting to spend the day in the park with him, hanging out at the ARF event. Maybe getting a hot dog at the concession stand for lunch (with Jake, of course. Sigh). He must not like me at all, I realized. And he's trying to just avoid me.

My heart sank, and my stomach bunched into knots.

I looked around to see if my friends had seen our interaction, and it was clear from the expressions on their faces that they had.

And right then I heard Jake cry, "Rocky!" and a huge dog came bounding over and knocked me nearly off my feet.

"Hey, boy!" exclaimed Jake.

Oh boy, I thought.

CHAPTER 4

Good Boy, Rocky!

𝓘 just don't get how my dad could ever have said this dog was on the smaller side," I said incredulously to Katie and Alexis. Rocky and Jake were snuggled up on a blanket on the grass while we squatted next to them, and Coach Mike and his new wife, Sandy, tossed a Frisbee back and forth nearby.

"Maybe he grew?" suggested Alexis.

"He certainly seems to love Jake," Katie said with a smile.

"And I love him!" Jake said happily.

"Um, Jake?" I said, peeking at the dog. "Rocky isn't a him, bud. He's a she."

"What?" Jake said, snapping upright. "He's a girl dog?!"

I laughed and nodded.

Jake stared accusatorily at Rocky. "You're a girl dog?!"

Rocky turned, looked at Jake, and panted.

There was a moment of tension when I actually thought Jake was going to get up and walk away in disgust. But finally he said, "That's okay, boy. I don't mind if you're a girl." And he flopped back down.

We all laughed.

"Phew!" I whispered to my friends.

My phone chirped with a message from Mia. How did the walkies go?

Oh boy. I hesitated. I wasn't in the mood to type some long reply. I could save the story for school on Monday. GR8, I texted, adding a dog and smiley icon.

There was a pause, and then Thank you!!! Big hugs to Jake!

I showed my phone to Jake, and he smiled sleepily and snuggled back into Rocky's side.

Katie was staring at Jake and Rocky. "If you dogsit that dog," she whispered, "you're going to have a heck of a time getting Jake to give her back."

I nodded. "You're right. But I'll let that be my parents' problem. It *would* be a good experience for him."

Alexis stood. "I'm going to go back over there and check on the ARF table."

"I'll come," I said.

"I'll stay with Jake," said Katie.

We walked back to the table. We had not yet discussed the Diego weirdness. I was worried if I started talking about it, I'd cry. I mean, it wasn't like we were supposed to go on a *date* and he stood me up, but it kind of was, in a way. Alexis was tactful enough to not bring it up. I could talk to her about anything, and I would, but in a little while. I still had to process it. He'd gone to speak with Mrs. Barnett and then left, flinging me a brisk wave on his way. I'd returned the wave halfheartedly and stared at him in total puzzlement as he'd walked away.

Now, at the ARF table, Mrs. Barnett and her crew were neatening up the display, restacking the leaflets. There were about two dozen cupcakes left, and Alexis freshened up the platter and removed wrappers and napkins to the trash.

"How's it going?" I asked Mrs. Barnett.

"Well, the cupcakes were a HUGE hit! Thank you! People loved them!" she said. "It was a big draw and a really good idea."

Alexis came back in time to hear the praise. We both smiled.

"It was Diego's idea, actually," offered Alexis.

"True," said Mrs. Barnett. "He's a great kid!"

"How about the pets?" I asked quickly, to change the subject. "Any interest?"

"We had lots of patters and holders, but no takers today," she said brightly. "It's okay. Pets are a huge commitment. People should be very sure before they take one home."

I looked sadly at the animals in the pens. Poor little guys. "So what happens now?"

She smiled. "We'll take them back and place some ads and spread the word and keep trying."

I climbed into the pen with the kitties. "Lex, wouldn't you like a sibling for Puff?"

Alexis climbed in next to me. "I totally would. I just know my parents wouldn't go for it. They love Puff, but they're not really cat people, you know? She trashed a chair in the living room with her claws, and my mom was *not* pleased."

I cringed. "Bummer." Alexis's house is super-neat, and all the furniture is in perfect condition. Unlike my house, where pets couldn't do much more damage than the boys already have. My mom always talks about her dreams for the day when we are all out of the house and she can redo everything in just the fabrics, rugs, and paint colors she loves, without thinking about them getting trashed.

Just then a tiny black-and-white kitten climbed up my calf, her needle-sharp claws digging through my pants and into my legs.

"Ow, little guy!" I cried. "I can see what you mean about the claws," I said to Alexis as I gently set aside the kitten and scooped up a small mostly grown tiger-striped cat. "But they are so darn cute. I actually like the adult ones better, in a way, though. They're mellower. I'd love to take this one home. Tigerlily, I'd call her." I smoothed her fur back from her face.

Alexis smiled and patted a silky all-black kitten. "Are you okay?" she asked, not looking at me.

I patted Tigerlily, who purred noisily on my lap. "Yeah. I guess so. Thanks. That was . . ."

"Weird. He was weird," Alexis said definitively. "Something was going on, for sure."

"Maybe he decided I'm annoying or something. I get it. I can be a total loser sometimes."

Alexis looked up and swatted me, laughing. "*Now* you're acting like a loser, but no one thinks of you as a loser. You're the hardest worker I know, you're totally relaxed around boys, you're sporty, you're smart, you're nice, and you're a model, for goodness sakes! What's not to love? Seriously, don't talk like that about yourself. It's awful!"

"Thanks, but I'm sure it's something I did or said."

"It was *definitely. Not. You.* Want me to go ask Mrs. Barnett what happened to him?" Alexis offered.

"No! What if she told him we'd been asking about him? I'd be mortified!"

"She doesn't seem like the type; she's so serious. Gossiping about teenagers seems a little beneath her. Plus, she obviously knows we're friends with him. He recommended us!"

"Well. I don't know. Let's just leave it alone for now."

"O-kaaay!" Alexis sang out. "Hey, look at Jake!"

Jake was throwing the Frisbee for Rocky, and Rocky was running and catching it in her mouth in midair and bringing it back to him, nearly knocking Jake over on the return. Jake was laughing his head off, and so were Katie, Mike, and Sandy, just from watching them. At one point, Jake basically tackled Rocky in a hug, and Rocky just stood and patiently absorbed it.

"I want to go ask those guys about Rocky," I said, gently depositing the sleeping Tigerlily on a bale of hay. "He's a pretty cool dog. I mean, she," I corrected myself.

"I'll come," offered Alexis. "By the way, I think you should get that cat."

I grinned. "I'd never thought of it before. We had a dog. But a cat of my own would be so cute." I looked at Tigerlily wistfully. "Maybe I'll ask my mom. But they are expensive to have. . . ."

"Tell me about it!" agreed Alexis. "But you do make plenty of money, Em."

We reached our little group, and I began asking Mike all about Rocky. It turns out her name was actually Roxy, but his niece, who was a toddler, couldn't pronounce it and said "Rocky" instead. Then it just stuck.

Mike told me she had been bred using a miniature poodle and a golden retriever, but the thing about these new kinds of breeds was you just never knew which genes were going to take and how. In this case, Rocky got her size from the retriever and her fur from the poodle. He'd seen other dogs from the same litter that were the opposite. Rocky had been small for the first nine months, and then she'd had a huge growth spurt.

"Is she done growing now?" I asked.

"Oh, I hope so!" moaned Sandy. "She's so giant in our tiny apartment. When she walks past the coffee table, her tail swipes everything right off. I can't even put my coffee down on it."

Mike laughed. "She probably wasn't the best purchase I ever made. It was an impulse buy, for Sandy's birthday. I saw an ad in the paper and just went to the people's house and bought her on the spot. She was just so darn cute!"

"She's a lot of work," said Sandy.

It was kind of a bummer. I could tell Sandy wasn't that into the dog. I thought about everything Mrs. Barnett had said about being ready. Then I thought about our family. I had to say, we were pretty ready, and we *were* set up for a dog. We had the fenced-in yard in the back; we also had invisible fencing all around in the front and back, from when we had Sissy; our house was already kind of trashed; someone was home a lot—the only times of day there wasn't always someone home was from nine to two thirty. Not so bad. And depending on my mom's shifts, she might be there one or two weekdays during those times, anyway. Plus, I knew a ton about dogs from my dog-walking business. And Jake was clearly eager. Taking stock of our situation made me feel good.

"We're getting a dog soon. Maybe for Jake's birthday next month," I said. I hoped it didn't sound braggy.

"Cool! What kind?" asked Mike.

"I don't know," I said. "We're kind of open to anything. A family dog. You know."

Mike watched Jake and Rocky as they happily romped around. "Would you get a puppy?" he asked.

I shrugged. "I don't think it has to be a puppy. I mean, puppies are the most fun, but if we couldn't find one we wanted right when we were ready, we might look at older dogs, maybe." I was saying all this as if my family had discussed it, when obviously we hadn't.

"Puppies are a lot of work," said Sandy, whom I now was starting to dislike. She was being so negative.

I nodded. "I know. I do a lot of dogsitting and dog-walking," I said. Oops. I shouldn't have said "dogsit." Nervously I glanced up to see Sandy and Mike exchange a glance.

"Hey, did your dad mention . . . ," began Mike.

I had to laugh. "My parents are discussing it. They are going to give you a call if the answer is yes," I said.

"It would be such a huge help. We'd really appreciate it," said Mike.

"Take my dog, please! You can keep her!" joked Sandy. Or at least I hoped she was joking.

"Ha-ha. Right," I said.

"Just let us know, okay?" said Mike.

"Sure thing. I'll tell them tonight that we saw you and how cute Rocky is."

"Thanks," said Mike, relieved. "It would be nice to have a break from her for a few days."

"Hmm," I said.

Jake came trooping over. "Emmy? I'm hungry. Can we go get lunch?"

"Sure," I said. "It looked like you were having a blast out there with your buddy."

"Yup. Rocky's my new best friend, right, boy?"

"Um, Rocky's actually a . . . ," Mike said, looking a little uncomfortable.

"Shh!" said Sandy. "Let him think whatever he wants!"

Jake looked up. "I know he's a girl. I just call him 'boy' 'cause that's what dogs are. Dogs are boys and cats are girls."

"*What?!* Where did you ever come up with that?" I demanded.

Jake shrugged. "I dunno. But that's why I think you should get one of those kitties over there! Let's go say bye before we leave." He stooped to hug Rocky one last time and then said, "See you at the game tomorrow, boy!"

And we all laughed and said our good-byes.

Katie and Alexis and I trailed behind Jake on the way back to the ARF table.

"Wow, that was pretty sad. That lady really doesn't like her dog," observed Alexis.

"I know! It made me so mad! I wanted to . . . I don't know. Put dog poop in her cupcake or something!" I said.

"Oooh, Emma! You go, girl!" teased Katie.

"Yes, she is one person who should not have a dog," agreed Alexis.

"Or at least not that dog," corrected Katie.

"Yeah, she should have a mean, snarly attack dog!" I said, laughing, and the others giggled.

Jake was in the cat pen, and the ARF people were loading up the dogs to go back to the shelter.

"Jake, didn't you like any of the doggies here?" I asked.

Jake looked over at the dog pen and then waved dismissively. "I like big fluffy dogs."

It was true; all the dogs in the pen were short-haired or smooth-coated. And they were all reasonably sized, unlike our friend Rocky.

"You know, Mom and Dad might not even let us get a dog," I began. "And if they do, it might have to be a small, practical dog. Like . . . a pug or something."

Jake laughed. "No way," he said. "I'm getting Rocky."

Uh-oh.

"Ha-ha. Rocky belongs to Mike and Sandy," I said.

"Hmmm," said Jake.

This was not good. But that's what parents are for, I reminded myself. It was *not* my problem.

Alexis was watching the dogs as they struggled, resisting being put back into their travel cages. The cats were more docile but still not psyched.

"I wonder what they think, being out here in the fresh air for the day, and all these people handling them, and then they just go back to the shelter. It's so sad," she said tragically.

I nodded. "But they'll find homes. You know they won't put them down. Mrs. Barnett said so."

"Yeah, but they might have to live there for a year and it's not"—Alexis lowered her voice— "exactly the lap of luxury."

"No kidding!" I agreed. "That's why I wanted to donate the cupcakes."

Alexis looked at me, stricken. "You were right. We're donating them. What was I thinking? These poor little critters. Come on. Let's tell Mrs. Barnett."

Mrs. Barnett tried to insist on paying, but she had never negotiated with Alexis Becker before. We didn't take a dime from them, though Mrs. Barnett did get Alexis to swear she would charge us full price next time. (Mrs. Barnett didn't know that Alexis is famous for crossing her toes in her shoes when she makes a promise she knows she won't keep, but I wasn't about to say anything.)

They finished loading the animals, and we wrapped up the remaining ten cupcakes for them to take back to their office and put in the break room. Mrs. Barnett and her staff thanked us profusely, and we waved sadly as they pulled away with their van filled with pets.

"Bye, doggies and kitties," I said softly.

Alexis looked ready to cry, which she never does. Katie *did* have a tear in her eye. "Oh, I wish my mom wasn't allergic!" she wailed.

"Jakey, why wouldn't you want to adopt one of those nice doggies that needs a home?" I said to him.

He was already walking away, completely untroubled by the ARF scenario.

"'Cause I'm getting Rocky!" he said.

I hated to admit it, but I could see why he wanted her so badly. They definitely had a bond. She just wasn't available for the taking.

CHAPTER 5

Tigerlily

I was looking through my Instagram when I got home, and I realized Diego had never posted anything about the ARF event today. That was weird. Usually, he did at least two posts prior to any ARF event and then a few photos from the actual event. It wasn't like I would ever ask him now, but it did seem odd.

At dinner, Jake and I told everyone about our dog day.

"Rocky is so cute, guys. We should totally dog-sit her," I said.

"Wait, *her*?" said my dad. "I thought it was a him?"

"Her." I explained about the name.

"Oh, that makes me feel better that it's a girl," said my mom. "Boy dogs like to mark their territories more, and that means peeing on furniture and all around the house. Not fun." She took a deep breath. "So, since we're on the topic, your dad and I did discuss it, and we think it would be fine to have Rocky come stay for a few days."

"Really? Yay!" Jake pumped his fists in the air. "You're the best parents ever! It will be so fun! You won't regret it!"

My mom laughed wearily. "Oh, I'm sure I'll regret it. But that's fine. We will have fun."

My dad agreed to call Mike after dinner. I pictured how thrilled Sandy would be and it annoyed me somehow. Rocky was a fantastic dog. You couldn't breed that kind of gentleness and personality, not to mention how cute she was. Sandy just didn't know how lucky she was. Or at least that's what I thought before Rocky arrived on Thursday.

Rocky took some getting used to, and that's putting it mildly. She was big and smelly, she liked to chew on shoes, it was true about her tail swiping across tables, and her favorite activity was waking people up in the morning. The first day of having her felt like a week.

But the second day, my dad put up two gates to keep her in the kitchen and family room only. We took all the stuff off the coffee table in the family room and made sure to leave our shoes inside the lockers in the mudroom. Sam brought some chew toys back from the mall after work, and she loved them. My dad gave her a bath in the mudroom's tub (he had to wear a bathing suit), and she loved that, too, and Rocky smelled great when she came out.

I saw my dad grimace at my mom afterward and then say, "I don't think that dog has had a bath in ages."

"Poor thing," my mom replied, helping to towel off Rocky. I saw my mom slip her an extra treat when she was done.

As for Jake taking care of the dog . . . Well, it quickly became clear what Jake's limitations were. He still refused to pick up dog poop. He did not want to walk Rocky alone. He gagged when he tried to feed her canned food. However, he did like snuggling with Rocky and brushing her fur, and he would throw the ball endlessly in the backyard for her, tiring her out for the night.

On the second afternoon, I came across my mom watching Jake and Rocky through the kitchen window, and I joined her.

"Pretty cute," my mom said.

Jake would throw the ball, and then Rocky would retrieve it and then drop it at Jake's feet. Jake would say something to Rocky, and Rocky would cock her head from side to side as Jake talked—it almost looked like they were having a conversation.

"Yeah, I guess. If he gets a dog, though, it's going to be a lot of work for everyone. 'Cause he won't do it on his own."

My mom nodded. "Mmm–hmmm," she agreed. "Maybe it needs to be everyone's dog."

That sounded okay (I knew who'd get stuck doing much of the walking and poop picking up: me!), but maybe if I got a cat, it would make me feel more generous toward the dog. I couldn't get Tigerlily off my mind. I kept googling cats and checking out Tigerlily's photo on the ARF website.

On Friday, Alexis agreed to go visit her with me after we baked Mona's cupcakes. Mia and Katie were going home instead of coming with us because we were having a sleepover Saturday at my house, so they wanted to get their homework done.

We got to ARF around four thirty, and they brought Tigerlily out to us in the glassed–in play area, known as the cat aquarium. She was pretty spunky, actually, chasing after a feather toy we found and playing with another cat. After a while, though, she crashed and snuggled into my lap for a nap. It was so cute.

"You should totally get her," said Alexis. Then something caught her eye outside the half-open door to the room. "Hey!" she said. "I think I just saw Diego go by."

"What?!" I whipped my head around, disturbing Tigerlily. "I haven't seen him all week. I wonder if he was even at school." I'd been hoping to run into him just one more time to confirm that he didn't like me. But then I hadn't seen him. Nor had he been posting anything about ARF at all. Tigerlily settled back to sleep as I soothed her with a pat.

"Will you pretty please go see for me if it's really him?" I asked Alexis.

"Chicken," she teased.

But then we saw him bolt past the door—Diego, for sure—and three people were rushing along behind him.

Alexis and I looked at each other.

"Is something going on out there?" I asked. "Seriously, you go check and I'll put back Tigerlily."

I gave the kitty some extra hugs and kisses and promised to try to come adopt her soon, but I wasn't sure that would happen. I was working on it. Slowly. I secured her in the cat aquarium and went out into the hall to see what was up.

Out in the hall there was a ruckus, and as I approached the front desk, there was a whole bunch of adults milling around frantically. Some were heading outside, and some were making phone calls, and Diego was there, running his fingers nervously through his hair. His back was to us, and I was embarrassed to call out his name. I nudged Alexis and gestured to her to approach him.

She shrugged and did. "Diego?" she said.

He spun around, but when he saw that it was Alexis, his face relaxed. "Oh, hey, Alexis." Then he noticed me, and he kind of turned away quickly.

My heart sank. It was official. He didn't like me.

"What's going on?" she asked.

I couldn't hear his reply, but I was beginning to get the gist of it from the people around me. Diego had been moving the dogs from the outside play area, back to their crates; but when he got upstairs, one was missing. Now, everyone was searching the neighborhood frantically and calling animal control and everything they could think of to find the poor little guy. His name was Bingo.

Diego dashed off, and Alexis came back over to me, her eyes wide.

"I know, I heard. And he obviously hates me, by the way. Ugh. What is wrong with—"

"Shush! Stop the self-criticism. I was going to tell you that Diego is covered, and I mean *covered*, in a rash of some sort. I bet that's why he was all bundled up in the park the other day. *And* why he doesn't want to see you. He probably loves you and is embarrassed!" Alexis smiled smugly. "Knew it!"

My jaw was hanging open. I couldn't think of what to say. I liked this possible version of events better than the Diego-not-liking-me version, but it was hard to process after days of thinking he didn't like me. "Huh" was all I could manage. I shook my head to clear it.

We saw Mrs. Barnett striding briskly down the hall, her mouth set in a grim line.

"Mrs. Barnett, can we help?" asked Alexis.

She looked surprised to see us there. "Oh. Thanks! Sure. Actually, you know what? I have a hunch that Bingo is somewhere in this building. Would you girls be willing to have a look around?"

Alexis and I readily agreed and set out.

We went from room to room—from vet checkup rooms, to shower rooms, to playrooms, to an operating room. . . .

"This place is huge!" I said.

"No wonder they need to raise so much money,"

said Alexis, in awe. "Their overhead and payroll must be staggering!"

I laughed and rolled my eyes at Alexis—also known as Ms. Business Lady.

By the time we had searched the place from top to bottom, running into a few other searchers along the way, we were confident that the dog was not in the building. We all regrouped at the front desk, and everyone quieted down while Mrs. Barnett stood in front to give an overview of the search and lay out the next steps. I watched Diego from the corner of my eye. He stood slightly apart from the group—besides the rash, he probably felt like an idiot for losing the dog. My heart went out to him.

But suddenly, as we were all standing there, the elevator doors opened with a loud *ding*.

I didn't turn to look, but some people did, and then there was an outcry.

"Bingo!" someone yelled.

I turned, and there in the elevator was the dog we'd all been looking for!

Diego ran to him and wrapped his arms around the dog's neck. The dog promptly licked Diego all over, and Diego laughed. It seemed that Diego had brought the dogs up in the elevator and gotten out on the second floor, but Bingo had stayed behind. When the doors closed, and with no one using the elevator for a while, the dog must have just lain down and taken a nap. The big mystery was why the doors had opened now. We'd never know.

"Maybe Bingo got hungry and decided the game of hide-and-seek was over!" someone said, and we laughed.

Diego was embarrassed but relieved. I had to speak with him; with everyone around, it felt less awkward.

I walked over. "Hey, Diego. I'm glad it all worked out," I said.

He seemed to instinctively duck his head, but then thought better of it, and he turned to face me. "Thanks. Me too," he said.

I could see now what Alexis had meant about the rash. It was all over his face and neck. I tried to keep my face neutral, but it did look pretty bad, though sort of like it was on its way to getting better.

Diego sighed and then gestured to his face. "By the way . . ."

Just then one of the vets interrupted him, and Diego looked at me helplessly, but with a smile, as he was drawn into yet another conversation about

Bingo, the Dog that Got Away. I smiled back and breathed a sigh of relief.

Okay, so he didn't hate me. That much I could tell. Phew. It was hard to say if he liked me at all, under the circumstances, but I'd settle for just not being *disliked* right now.

"Should we head home?" Alexis asked.

I nodded. "I feel so bad about leaving Tigerlily here, though."

"Talk to your parents tonight!" Alexis said in exasperation. "Maybe they'll let you come get her tomorrow!"

"Hmm. Probably not tomorrow, with Rocky staying through the weekend," I said. "But I will."

Just as we had retrieved our jackets and were getting ready to walk out the door, Mrs. Barnett stopped us. "Girls! Thanks for your help with the search today." She smiled and shook her head in wonder. "I always think I've seen it all, and then something like this happens!"

We laughed.

"Listen, we're going to do another park event next weekend, and we'd love you to bake for us. We were also thinking it might be fun to have some doggy cupcakes. Is that something you could figure out how to do, also?"

"Sure! Let us take a crack at it! It'll be a whole new area for us," Alexis said heartily. "Petcakes!"

"Sounds great," I agreed. "Thanks."

Mrs. Barnett smiled. "Great. Good luck, and whatever you do, don't sample the results."

We laughed again and Alexis and I headed on our way.

Outside, Alexis moaned. "Oh no! What did we just get ourselves into?"

I patted her arm and said, "Product line extension. Isn't that what you entrepreneurs call it?"

"Oh boy. Why did I ever teach you about this stuff?" she said mock-regretfully. "And how do you even remember it?"

"Steel trap," I whispered, pointing to my head.

That night at dinner, I brought up Tigerlily.

"You can't get a cat, Emmy! I'm getting a dog!" protested Jake. "Cats and dogs fight!"

"Like cats and dogs," said Matt under his breath.

"Ha-ha," I said to Matt. "Well, that may be true of *some* cats and dogs," I said to Jake. "But our cat and dog will get along. Especially because your dog will probably be a puppy, and it makes it easier if they are younger when they meet."

"Rocky's not a puppy!" protested Jake.

"Oh, brother. Mom! He thinks we're keeping Rocky. What are we going to do?"

"But Tigerlily isn't a kitten, is she, sweetheart?" asked my mom, pointedly ignoring the Rocky issue. She'd gotten tired—we'd all gotten tired—of explaining to Jake that Rocky wasn't our dog.

Rats. "No . . . she's not a kitten." I shook my head. "But she's young. Maybe a teenager."

"We'll discuss it," said my dad. "It's a lot to go from *no* animals to *two* animals, all at once. And next thing I know, Matt and Sam are going to want something too."

"I want a snake!" Matt said enthusiastically, looking up from his plate. "A huge one, like a boa constrictor or something. The kind that eats . . . puppies!"

"And teenage cats!" Sam added mischievously.

Jake shrieked, playing right into their hands, but I just rolled my eyes.

"We are *not* having a snake in this house," my mother said empathically. "No way, mister!"

Matt laughed. "Just kidding. I want mice, anyway. So cute, so tiny . . ."

My mother moaned. "Not mice, either! No rodents!"

"A tarantula?" teased Matt.

"Very funny, Matthew," said my mom sarcasti-cally. *"Not!"*

"So what do you think about Tigerlily?" I pressed.

"Why don't we go see her tomorrow?" said my dad. "And I'll talk to the people at ARF about cats and dogs and expenses and everything." He passed his hand over his face wearily. "What am I getting myself into?" he muttered.

"Great!" I cried, ignoring his fears. "Can the Cupcakers come with us?"

He nodded. "The Cupcakers can come. Of course."

CHAPTER 6

Emergency!

$\mathcal{K}$atie, Mia, and Alexis came over right after lunch on Saturday. They all were eager to see Rocky and check out what our house was like with a dog in it. All my friends were excited for Jake to get a dog, and they were psyched for me, too. Of course, every conversation with Jake about dogs ended with him exclaiming he was keeping Rocky, and he didn't understand what all these puppy questions were about. I rolled my eyes so much, they were sore.

Besides the dog viewing, Katie had googled a bunch of doggy cupcake recipes for us to try out. We decided to make two different kinds of batches and let them cool while we went to ARF to see Tigerlily. We would test out one of each kind of cupcake on Rocky when we got home to see which one she preferred.

The first batch was vegetarian. It had shredded carrots and applesauce and oats and other veggie things. The second batch was peanut butter and had a cream-cheese-and-yogurt frosting with crumbled bacon.

"If I were a dog, I'd go for the bacon one," Matt said, passing through on the way home from a soccer game.

Alexis laughed, teasing him. "Gee, there's a surprise!" Matt was famous for loving our salted caramel and bacon cupcakes. "I wouldn't even put it past you to try one of these!"

"Woof!" barked Matt, making Alexis giggle hysterically.

The rest of us rolled our eyes at one another, but we were smiling.

Soon, the cupcakes and frostings were finished, and we put everything on the kitchen counter to come to room temperature while we were gone. There were forty-eight cupcakes and two big bowls of frosting. If Rocky thought they were tasty, we'd drop them by ARF tomorrow as a donation and then make up a new batch of the favorite for the event next weekend.

As we left, my mom was going to do her yoga upstairs, and Jake and Rocky were watching a movie until it was time for him to go to a birthday party. Sam was at work, and Matt had to go shower and meet his study group.

We set out for ARF in a cheerful mood. I was excited to see Tigerlily and hoped to convince my dad that I should get her. I was also hoping I might see Diego at ARF while we were there. Little did I know who I'd end up seeing.

The good news about my dad is that he is a major softy when it comes to animals. His grandparents had a farm when he was growing up, and he used to go out and stay with them. He really loved taking care of their "livestock," as he annoyingly calls their animals.

The Cupcakers and my dad and I were let into the cat aquarium while a volunteer went to get Tigerlily for us. There was another young family there playing with an adorable black-and-white kitten. It was tiny! But I watched it do what the kitten had done to me the other day—it climbed up the little girl's leg, and she cried out in pain.

"Kittens are overrated," I whispered to our group. "I actually think they're kind of gross, too,"

I joked. "Their little claws are so sharp, and their butts are always poopy. . . ."

"Eeeew!" squealed Mia, who is not a cat person at all.

"How can you not like kittens?" Alexis asked. "I mean, seriously, who doesn't like kittens? What else don't you like? Rainbows? Birthday parties? Ice cream?"

"Hate 'em." I grinned.

"Here she is!" announced the volunteer, who arrived with a sleepy-looking Tigerlily in her arms. I was sitting on the floor, and she placed her gently in my arms and Tigerlily nestled right into the crook of my arm and fell back asleep.

"Awww!" said Katie. "She loves you. You're her mommy!"

"Isn't she cute, Dad?" I asked, smiling up at my father.

"Adorable," he agreed. "Will you let me hold her next?"

I snuggled with her for a minute and then handed her over. My dad took her and competently folded her into his arms and began patting her head. She purred loudly, like a machine.

"Boy, you sure know your way around a cat!" I teased.

"Years of practice on the barn cats," bragged my dad.

"Hey, it's the Cupcake Club!" Mrs. Barnett said, arriving at the cat aquarium.

We introduced her to my dad, and the timing was perfect. Mrs. Barnett and my dad fell into a serious conversation about the financial and practical requirements of cat (and dog) ownership, and she shared advice with him on how best to introduce two pets to each other. It was interesting to listen to what she said; she knew a lot about animal behavior. I thought she was just an administrator, but it turned out she'd been an animal sciences major in college. She had wanted to be a vet but got married and had kids early and decided not to finish the program. Now, she was going to school at night to finish up her degree and then apply to veterinary school. It sounded like a ton of work, but the way her eyes lit up when she talked about it was pretty noticeable.

The good news about what Mrs. Barnett said was that it was probably better to get the cat first. She advised us to have the cat for two weeks or so, to get her used to the house and all of us, and then we could add a dog. We would need to proceed with keeping them separate at first and gradually introducing them, with the dog on a leash, and then after about two weeks, we could let them just interact unrestricted.

Mrs. Barnett explained that if we used the vets at ARF, it would be cheaper than going with a fancy, independent vet. She said Tigerlily had already been spayed, so she couldn't have kittens, so that was one expense we wouldn't have to worry about. All animals who were taken in by ARF were spayed or neutered by them, so that they couldn't produce any more unwanted pets.

Beyond the yearly checkup and shots were the food and cat litter expenses. If we kept to grocery store brands of food and litter, we could keep prices down on those, too. Furthermore, she said if we were planning on letting the cat be an indoor-outdoor cat, it would even cut down on the litter costs because the cat would go to the bathroom outdoors much of the time. Our only additional cost would be flea and tick prevention.

My dad was nodding along. "That doesn't sound too bad."

"It's really not," agreed Mrs. Barnett. "I find cats the best family pets. They adapt easily, they deliver a lot of snuggles, and they're quite easy to care for. And—don't tell anyone I ever said this because I'm not supposed to admit it, but—you can even leave them alone for a day or two without needing someone to look after them." She gave us a big wink.

"Sounds like a better choice than a dog," my dad said with a sigh.

"Well, you just need to find the right dog for your family," said Mrs. Barnett. "Some dogs are quite low maintenance. Other dogs require a lot of supervision. . . ."

Just then my mom came running into the cat aquarium. Her hair was uncharacteristically wet and up in a bun, and she was in her yoga clothes. "Honey! I need your help!" she called to my dad.

"Mom? Wh-what are you . . . ?" I sputtered.

"It's Rocky! She ate all the cupcakes and frosting and everything, and she is so sick. . . . We're through here at the emergency entrance."

My dad and Mrs. Barnett jumped up and ran to follow her.

The Cupcakers and I exchanged alarmed looks.

"I feel so bad!" I moaned. "Rocky binged on our cupcakes and got sick."

"They couldn't be bad for her?" said Katie.

"No, she just ate too much!" said Mia. "Forty-eight cupcakes and two bowls of frosting? Gross!"

"Em, do you want me to keep Tigerlily so you can go see what happened?" asked Alexis, her face tight with worry.

"Sure. Thanks," I said, and gently handed over the cat and then scrambled out to see what was going on.

They had put Rocky on a gurney and were wheeling her into an examining area. Jake had tears streaming down his face, and my mom looked pretty choked up too. My dad's mouth was set in a grim line.

Rocky was lying on her side, panting heavily. Every so often she'd convulse a little, like she wanted to be sick, but there was nothing left in her.

The vet and a nurse took over. "Hey, girl, you're going to be okay! Don't worry," the vet said in a soothing voice. "I bet you feel pretty awful right now, though." She gave Rocky long, slow pats as she examined her. "You are a patient puppy!"

"Yes, she really is," agreed my dad.

"How old is she?" asked the vet.

"We think she's about fifteen months," said my dad.

"We're only dogsitting her for the weekend," said my mom. "She's not ours."

"Yet!" added Jake.

The nurse smiled down at him.

The vet was stroking Rocky's abdomen, and she paused, a puzzled look on her face. She kept reaching and re-feeling the same area. "Bill," she called to the nurse. "Can you bring an ultrasound machine, as well as an IV with a small bag of anti-nausea fluids and some electrolytes, please?"

The nurse nodded and then ducked out of the room as the vet continued her exam, looking in Rocky's eyes and mouth. I was still stuck on the IV. I do not do well with needles, and I was not going to be able to hang around for this.

"Is she going to be okay?" I asked the vet.

"Sure. This kind of thing is very common. Sweet dog," she said, smoothing Rocky's hair away from her eyes. "We'll get her on some electrolytes . . . like doggy Gatorade," she said to Jake with a smile. "And a little medication to settle her tummy, and she'll be fine in no time. She'll have to take it easy for the rest of the weekend, though. And very plain dry food. No treats," added the vet.

Rocky lifted her head as she heard the word "treat," and we laughed.

"There is just one more thing I want to check quickly . . . ," said the vet as the nurse came back with the equipment the vet had requested.

"This is where I exit . . . ," I said with a nervous laugh. I did not want to faint at ARF.

"Okay, sweetheart. We'll come find you when we're finished," offered my mom.

Just as I headed out of the emergency area, who did I bump right into but Diego!

"Oh, hi!" he said with a grin. "What are you doing here?"

His rash was noticeably better than the day before, and I saw that he didn't really duck his head like yesterday, nor was he super–covered up.

I explained about Rocky, and his eyes grew wide. "I'll have to be more careful when I eat your cupcakes!" he teased.

I swatted him. "Very funny. It's 'cause she ate too many!"

He looked at me mock-seriously. "That could happen to me too!"

"Well, then, be careful," I said. "We don't need you coming in here on a gurney!"

"Speaking of which, I meant to tell you . . . I'm sorry I've been so weird and kind of avoiding everyone. I had . . . I got all these flea bites from a new batch of kittens they brought in. And then I put on this cream, and I had an allergic reaction to the cream, and I broke out in this horrible rash all over.... It was so embarrassing. I had to miss school. It really hurt."

"Wow! That's awful!" I said. "I was wondering. I mean . . ." Ugh. I didn't want him to know I'd been hurt by what felt like his avoiding me.

"Yeah. That day at the park. I had been looking forward to it, so then I was really annoyed and embarrassed and whatever. I never got a chance to promote it or post any pics from the event. I was so bummed that I missed it. I heard it went really well."

"Yeah, it did," I agreed. "Also, I met Tigerlily that day. She's the cat I'm here to see. I really want to adopt her."

"Wait, so you guys are getting a dog *and* a cat? At the same time?"

I nodded. "I think so. More or less."

"You are so lucky. And that's a good strategy, by the way. Having them both be new to the house will keep things on a level playing field for them, so they aren't too territorial."

"Yup. Want to come see her?" I asked, and he agreed.

"I don't have any pets," Diego confessed as we walked down the hall to the adoption area.

"What?!" I was shocked. "I thought you'd be Dr. Doolittle, surrounded by your adoring flock of pets!"

But he was shaking his head. "My dad and my sister are superallergic to everything, so I even have to take off my clothes in the laundry room and put them right in the hamper after I've been here."

"*Wow!* Crazy!" I said. "I had no idea."

"Yup. That's why I volunteer here. My mom finally got tired of me complaining and suggested that if I loved animals so much, I should put my money where my mouth is, or whatever the expression is. So I showed up here, and it's been great! I think I'll probably become a vet when I'm older."

"That's so cool. You're lucky to know what you want to be when you grow up."

He smiled, and his even white teeth dazzled me. "I want to be a professional cupcake taster, actually."

I laughed. "Welcome aboard!" I said, and we headed in to meet my friends.

We hung out for about an hour, playing with Tigerlily and some of her friends that Diego brought down. He also got us a bunch of toys and some treats, and it was really fun. By the end of the hour, it was clear Tigerlily knew she was mine. She kept returning to

81

me like I was her home base. It was so cute. All I had to do now was officially adopt her.

Finally, my dad poked in his head. "Sorry, gang. You won't believe the news about Rocky! I can run you home, now, if you're ready. Em, let's decide about Tigerlily tonight, and if we're getting her, it will have to be tomorrow, after Rocky goes home, okay?"

I wanted to whine and stamp my foot and insist that Tigerlily come home with me today, but I couldn't do it in front of Diego and my friends. Plus, I felt a little bad for my dad. He looked stressed.

"Okay," I agreed.

"I'll put her back for you," offered Diego. "And I'll check on her all day today and take her out to play tomorrow while I'm here, okay?"

I nodded. "That's really nice. Thanks so much, Diego." I gave the kitty a hug and kiss and whispered that I'd see her tomorrow, for sure. I wished I could hug Diego, too. He was so nice.

Instead, I turned to my dad. "What's the news about Rocky? Good or bad?"

He laughed and turned to face us all. "I'm not sure. Rocky's going to have puppies!"

CHAPTER 7

Puppies!

$\mathcal{M}$y dad called Coach Mike with the news when we got home. I wished I could have listened in. I was sure Mike would be floored by the news. The vet had done an ultrasound and could see four puppies, maybe five, in Rocky's abdomen. That was a lot of puppies. The way I saw it was as great news: If Jake couldn't have *Rocky*, at least he could have one of her kids!

When my dad hung up, I ran out from the family room to get the scoop on the call.

"What did Mike say? Could he believe it?"

My dad shook his head. "He was not very happy about it. They'd been searching everywhere this weekend for a rental that would allow dogs, and they couldn't find anything down there.

They're really getting stressed, and now this on top of it. I asked him nicely why he hadn't had her spayed, and he said his wife hadn't wanted to spend the money, and they thought Rocky was still too young to get pregnant."

Rocky was due to have her puppies in two weeks.

"Wow. Lots of baby doodles! So what are they going to do?" I asked. "What are they going to *doodle*?" I giggled.

My dad laughed too, but then he grew serious. "He didn't know. I could hear his wife in the background. She was kind of upset. Freaking out, actually. He said he'd have to call me back. Poor kid."

"Wow. Some people just really shouldn't have dogs," I said.

"I know," agreed my dad.

"I'm going to give the Cupcakers the update," I said, returning to the family room, where we were making beaded bracelets and eating popcorn while we watched one of Alexis's required dance shows before we turned on a movie.

Meanwhile, Jake had been allowed to bring Rocky and her huge bed up to his room, and he was literally holding a vigil at her bedside, watching her every breath. It was pretty cute. I'd never seen him act so responsible before. Usually, he just loses interest in things after a little bit. Rocky was better but pretty wiped out from her ordeal. The vet said we'd be surprised by how quickly she'd bounce back, though.

Back in the family room, my friends were dismayed by Mike's reaction to Rocky's news.

"It's too bad they're not into that dog. If she were my dog, I would be obsessed," said Katie.

"I think Jake and that dog have a real bond too," I mused.

"Totally," Alexis agreed, tearing her eyes away from the TV for a minute.

"Oh, that little Jakey is so cute," said Mia. "I wish I could adopt *him* and get *him* some toys and treats and take him home to live with me!"

"Be my guest!" I offered, but they all scolded me.

"You're so lucky to have that little guy," said Katie. "I wish I had someone else in my house. It's so quiet and lonely whenever I get home. My mom's at work, and it's just me!"

"Okay: *You* need a *dog*!" Mia said decisively, pointing her finger at Katie.

Katie laughed. "Oh, but my mom's allergic. You

know that! That's why I could never have a pet."

"Doodles are hypoallergenic, supposedly," I said with a shrug.

"Really?" said Katie. "Maybe I'll have my mom come in and play with Rocky tomorrow when she picks me up."

"You should!" I agreed. "Wouldn't it be awesome if she wasn't allergic?"

"Yeah," Katie said dreamily.

"I'll cross my fingers," I said.

Rocky was fit as a fiddle the next day. We made some more petcakes and decided I'd drop them at ARF for taste testing later in the afternoon, when my dad and I went to see Tigerlily. Despite the events of the previous day, Rocky seemed very interested in sampling the petcakes, which we thought was a good sign. My mother, however, forbade us from giving her any.

"I do *not* need that dog getting sick again. It was not a pretty sight or an easy cleanup," she said, her nose wrinkling in distaste.

"Get used to it, Mom," I joked. "When Jake gets his puppy, that little critter's going to make lots of messes."

My mom sighed. "I know. At least Rocky's

housebroken. Mike did a good job training her."

Just then Jake walked into the kitchen.

I nodded. "Yeah, Rocky also sits and stays."

"And shakes! I taught her last night. Watch!" said Jake. Then he turned to the dog. "Rocky, sit!" Rocky sat. "Okay, Rocky . . . shake!" Jake put out his hand, and Rocky lifted her paw and put it in Jake's hand. Everyone cheered.

I was amazed. "You taught her that? How?"

Jake smiled proudly. "I googled it. Then I did what the lady in the video said."

"Wow, Jake. That's impressive. Can I try?"

He let me, and sure enough, Rocky shook for me. Everyone took turns, and then we were all patting Jake on the back.

"Great job, Jakey!" said Mia.

"I might become a dog trainer for the Big Apple Circus when I'm older. Like the guy in *Stay*," he said matter-of-factly. "Next, I'm going to teach her to play dead. You just make a gun with your finger and point it at her and say, 'Bang, bang!,' and she'll fall on the floor and lie on her side."

"Jake! That sounds awful!" said my mom, which made him grin even more.

"Well, you'd better get going on it because Mike is coming to pick her up in two hours," I reminded him. Then I felt bad—I knew how much he loved Rocky.

Jake's face fell. "I don't want Rocky to leave."

"I know, me neither," agreed Alexis.

My mom lifted her eyebrows and sighed. "She *is* a sweet dog."

"That's why we should keep her!" said Jake. "Everybody loves you, boy," he said, hugging Rocky's neck.

"Girl," I corrected.

"Jake, are you going to get one of Rocky's puppies?" asked Katie.

"Maybe!" my mom said brightly, in that tone of voice moms use for when they're speaking on behalf of kids who are right in front of them.

Jake scowled. "No."

"Oh!" said Katie, taken aback. She looked at me in confusion. "I thought . . . ?"

I shrugged. "Who knows? *I* think we should get one." I thought Jake would be thrilled.

"Come on, boy, let's go outside and work on your tricks," said Jake, and they went out into the fenced backyard.

"Was it something I said?" joked Katie.

My mom looked thoughtful. "He really is devoted to that dog."

"When he sees the puppies, he'll fall in love. Don't worry, Mom. And he'll get the pick of the litter, I'm sure. I just hope Mike and Sandy don't move before the puppies are born."

Katie's mom came to pick her up a little later, and we rushed to the car in the driveway, dragged her out, and brought her in to meet Rocky.

"Uh-oh!" My mom laughed when she saw what was going on. "Puppy fever is already striking!"

Mrs. Brown laughed. "Good thing I brought my inhaler!" she cried as we pulled her through the kitchen and out to the yard.

Mrs. Brown was a good sport about it. She sat on the patio and patted Rocky and listened to Katie enumerate the many reasons why they should get a (hypoallergenic) dog. Mrs. Brown didn't seem to have any reactions to Rocky, which she said was unusual. When it was really time for them to leave, she offered to drop off Alexis and Mia and said she and Katie would go home to "begin a conversation" about dogs. Katie was ecstatic, and I hugged her extra hard when she left.

"Good luck!" I whispered in her ear.

"You too!" she replied, referring to Tigerlily.

After everyone had left, my parents and I sat down to have a serious conversation about Tigerlily.

I crossed my fingers and put them in my pockets so my parents couldn't see.

"It's a little unplanned. I mean, we've never been a cat family. I don't know much about cats as pets," said my mom.

"It seems pretty easy," my dad said with a shrug. "I spoke to Linda Barnett about it at length at ARF yesterday."

"I can do it all," I offered. "I'll take care of her. I'll pay for her food and litter and the vet. I earn enough money to cover it. I would just love to have my own little girl kitty who could sleep on my bed and wait for me to come home from school. It would be so cozy!"

My mom laughed. "I can see the appeal."

"She *is* a sweet cat," said my dad, looking at me. "So what do you say?"

My parents looked at each other. "Okay by me, I guess," relented my mom. "You'll take care of her. I don't mind buying the supplies, but you deal with her shots and the vet and all that, deal?"

"Ugh. Shots?" I said.

My mom looked at me. "You don't have to *watch*. You just have to bring her once a year, and stay on top of it. I just can't add lots of new schedules to my life if we're also getting a dog."

"Okay." It seemed like a small price to pay. "Dad?"

"Great. Sounds good to me." He stood, and we were about to set off when the doorbell rang.

"Oh! There's Mike to pick up Rocky, I bet," said my dad. "This might take a few minutes."

A few minutes turned out to be almost an hour! I was so impatient, I thought I'd burst! Rocky had been thrilled to see Mike, and I actually felt bad for Jake at the reception she gave Mike. Mike was happy to see her too, and he got down on the floor to hug her. It almost looked like he was crying a little. I guess if I'd been away from my dog for a few days, I might cry a little when I saw her again. Maybe?

But then Mike asked if he and my parents could have a chat in private, and Jake got a worried look on his face. As they all went out to the living room to talk, Jake turned to me, pale as a sheet. "Is Mike mad at me that Rocky got sick? He's going to say I did a bad job for letting her get at those cupcakes. But I didn't know! I was watching a movie, and she got up and I didn't even notice she was gone for so long." He sat down heavily on a kitchen chair and put his head in his hands. "He must be really mad. Do you think they'll punish me? Maybe he'll bench me at the next game. Ooooh!" Jake moaned.

I knelt down next to him. "Jake! Dude, get a grip! It's not your fault that Rocky got sick. It's my fault for not thinking about Rocky when we left the cupcakes out to cool. He should bench *me* if he's going to bench anyone!" I laughed.

Jake scowled at me through his hands. "*You're* not even on the *team*," he said icily.

"Listen," I said, patting his shoulder. "You took great care of Rocky this week. She could not have been happier or healthier, except for the cupcake thing, which wasn't your fault. And if it weren't for the cupcakes, we wouldn't have even found out that Rocky was pregnant! Think of that! No one would have known to take care of her health in the special ways you do when a dog is going to have puppies. It actually worked out great." I rubbed his leg. "Don't be so hard on yourself, little guy. You're a good kid!"

Jake smiled up at me. "Thanks. You're a good kid too, Emmy!" He threw his arms around me and gave me a big hug. It was so adorable. If Mia and Katie could see me now, they'd be green with envy. I guess they were right. Jake was pretty sweet sometimes. And then he said, "And when Rocky comes to live with us, I'll let her sleep on your bed sometimes."

Oh, brother. When was this kid going to learn?

As it turned out, though, Jake was sort of right.

Coach Mike had come to plead with my parents to keep Rocky through when she had the puppies and they were old enough to leave her. Sandy was insistent that they could not move into a new home in a new state with new jobs and with a dog that was about to give birth at any minute. I had to kind of agree with her, even though I didn't like her very much. This was probably all great for her—she got rid of the dog for a couple of months and didn't have to deal with any of the messy stuff.

My parents agreed, mostly because they felt sorry for Rocky. Plus, they knew how happy it would make Jake. I think they even offered to keep her for good, but Mike just couldn't give her up. I wasn't supposed to know that part because they really didn't want Jake to know that they had tried and failed to get Rocky for him.

Instead, they spun it that Coach Mike was so impressed by Jake's tender loving care of Rocky, he wanted us to be the ones to help her become a mother.

"What a guy," Matt said sarcastically when he heard the news. "We do all the dirty work, and he gets his dog back. What's he going to do with the puppies?"

My mom and dad looked at each other, aghast.

"We didn't get that far!" said my dad.

"Oh no!" said my mom.

"*Seriously*, people?" I said.

Matt just shook his head. "There's a sucker born every minute."

"Can we go get my cat now, please?"

And my parents looked at each other again and then collapsed into helpless laughter. Parents are so weird sometimes.

CHAPTER 8

Tigerlex

It's official: Tigerlily Alexis Taylor has come home to live with me!

Last night I came home with her, and Matt, the computer graphics wiz, helped me make little adoption announcements with her photo, and a little kitty paw print on them. All in pink. It is so cute. I'm going to hand them out to my friends at school today, and I know they'll think it's hilarious.

Tigerlily slept on my bed for the whole night, in a warm little ball by my feet. It was the best night ever. We were supposed to keep her in just one room for her first night, but she was too curious, so she got out and explored the whole house when I was in the shower. She knows how to open doors, by the way. She is a genius kitty. She stands on her hind legs and lifts her front paws up on either side of a doorknob and then moves her paws up and down until the knob turns. I'm going to video it and send it in to *The World's Funniest Home Videos*.

We were supposed to keep her upstairs and away from Rocky and blah, blah, blah, but it just wasn't realistic in this household. And anyway, it turned out the two critters liked each other! There was lots of sniffing and checking each other out last night, but nobody barked or hissed or anything. I think it's good that we have those gates to keep Rocky in the kitchen, though. It allows Tigerlily to have the rest of the house to herself.

So this morning, Tigerlily followed me down into the kitchen, and Rocky was lying on her bed in a warm, sunny corner. My mom had already sent her outside to do her business and she had eaten, so she was all snoozy. Tigerlily walked right over to her, bold as you please, and gave her a good sniffing. Rocky didn't even twitch! She just opened one eye lazily and checked out TL and then went back to sleep.

"Mom! Did you see that?!" I cried.

"Mmmm-hmm! Incredible!" she murmured, taking a sip of her coffee.

Right then, Tigerlily gave Rocky a little bat on the snout, and Rocky hopped up and started chasing her around the kitchen. Tigerlily ran like a streak and flew over the gate to the hall and disappeared. Rocky stood there, panting and staring at us, as if to say, *Can you believe the nerve of that one?*

"Maybe they were just playing?" I said to my mom.

"Uh-huh, whatever you say," she said with a smile. She had to see how cute they were together!

I settled onto a stool at the counter for breakfast, which my mom served up: scrambled eggs, a piece of buttered whole wheat toast, and some cut-up apples with cinnamon on them. While I munched, my mom and I talked about plans for Rocky's upcoming motherhood.

"I need to call the vet today at ARF to find out about scheduling doctor's appointments for her and what else we need to do. I think we have about two weeks or so. We have to up her calcium intake; I think I read somewhere to give her cottage cheese. We also need to make her a special bed; I looked it up online," said my mom.

"Oh, my friends and I could help with that!" I said. "We could make it supercozy."

"Great!" said my mom. "Thanks. You'll just have to involve Jake because, you know . . ."

"He's a spoiled brat?" I said sweetly.

My mom waved a dish towel menacingly at me. "He thinks she's his," my mom said firmly.

"She's *everyone's* while she's here. And she's really *Mike's*!" I said.

"Rocky!" cried Jake, rolling into the kitchen. He scrambled to her side and nestled in next to her on her doggy bed.

"Gross, Jake!" I said, wrinkling my nose. "That bed is so hairy and dirty!"

"I think it's beautiful, like Rocky," he replied.

I looked at my mom.

She shrugged. "It's like every day is Christmas for him with her here. It's so sweet," she said.

I stood and put my plate and glass in the dishwasher, then headed up to change for school. "Whatever you say, lady!" I said.

The remaining weeks of Rocky's pregnancy passed quickly. The weather grew cooler and ARF hosted two more events at the park. We Cupcakers baked petcakes for pups and cats, and our original masterpieces, for both events. Alexis charged half price—enough to cover our expenses—and everyone was happy. They got a deal, and we didn't lose any money. It all worked out.

The best part for me was getting to be friends with Diego. I am still majorly crushing on him, but I have to say first that we are officially friends. I have gone to ARF a few times with him to work as a volunteer. We walk the dogs (which I am obviously very qualified for), clean out the cat boxes (ditto), and play with the animals in the yard and the cat aquarium.

Diego has done a lot more posting of photos, and Mrs. Barnett says that his publicity is directly responsible for the adoption of a cat and a puppy at the event last week. I am so proud of him. Also, he has a new plan to subject his dad and his sister to Rocky before the puppies come, just in case they might not be allergic, like Mrs. Brown.

But over the last few weeks, Jake has been the most impressive one of all. He makes certain to feed Rocky her cottage cheese every day, even though she doesn't really like it. He talks Rocky into taking a walk, even when she doesn't want to go out, because the vet cautioned us not to let Rocky gain too much weight, or the birth could get difficult for her. Jake also helped build a bed out of a huge refrigerator box that my dad got from a friend at work, who'd just had a new fridge delivered. They laid it on its side, length-wise, cut off the top and part of a side, and then lined it with old foam cushion inserts from our old patio furniture, covered in plastic sheeting, and topped with clean old towels. I have to admit, I'd sleep in there if I were a dog. Jake put in a couple of Rocky's rag toys and taped up a huge photo of himself on the wall, which is kind of hilarious. It's in the mudroom, where she can access it when she needs to deliver the babies.

My parents were so proud of him that after the second week of Rocky's visit, they sat him down and told him my mom had done the research and bought tickets to the Big Apple Circus! Jake could bring two friends and they could each have a copy of *Stay*. After the circus, they could have pupcakes and a sleepover.

Jake was so happy, I wish I had videoed it for Mia and Katie! He kept laughing and clapping, falling over on the couch, shouting, "Yessssss!" And then he ran to tell Rocky. There were a couple of agonizing days afterward with him try-ing to decide who to pick (including one day when he was firm in the opinion that his guests should be me and Mia), but he finally settled on two easygoing friends whose parents were also close friends of my parents. I'm sure my parents nudged him in this direction, but it was a smart choice. They'd have a good time, all of them.

The day of the birthday party arrived, and Jake's friends were dropped off for the outing and sleepover. They brought their bags and gifts into the kitchen and stowed everything in the mud-room, and then they set out for the show in the city.

My older brothers and I were on our own for the afternoon and evening, with no friends allowed over since my parents were out of town. My dad left money for us to have a couple of pizzas deliv-ered (my older brothers could eat a whole pie each, so I'd have to fight for my two slices). As my mom left, she said, "Em, call me if you need me, okay?"

I waved her off. "We're *fine*, Mom! Seriously, go! Have fun with the doggie clowns!"

I went to my room to play with TL and a new little mouse toy Diego had brought to school for me to give to her. It was so sweet, and she loved it. I snapped a pic with my phone and texted it to him. He replied right back, Cool cat! and I smiled. Suddenly, Tigerlily sat bolt upright, her ears perked and twitching. I stopped to listen, and there was a ruckus coming from downstairs.

I stood up and went to the stair landing. "Guys?" I called down to Matt and Sam. But they had the football game on so loud that they couldn't hear me.

There was some kind of thrashing coming from the kitchen.

"Darn them!" I muttered. "I'll be right back, Tigerlex!" I called. That was my new nickname for her, after her godmother, Alexis, of course.

The noise was coming from the mudroom and had grown quite loud by the time I was there.

"Rocky?" I called anxiously as I approached the room. Was it time? Were we going to have to deliver these puppies all by ourselves?!

"Rocky?" I whispered.

The thrashing stopped. I peeked my head around the corner and found that Rocky had ripped open the gifts from Jake's friends, shredded the paper, and was now having her way with the gifts that had been inside.

Lucky for Rocky, they were dog gifts. Jake's friends knew that he was majorly into Rocky and that he'd be getting a puppy soon, so they'd bought him dog toys and treats. Cute!

Rocky looked at me guiltily, and I wagged my finger at her. "Bad dog!" I said, gathering up the paper and gently removing one of the toys from her mouth. I set the gifts on a high shelf in one of the lockers and went to throw away the paper. Usually, Rocky follows us to the garbage and recycling area in the kitchen hoping for some dropped food, but when I turned back, she wasn't there.

"Rocky?" I called.

I dumped the paper in the recycling bin and retraced my steps to the mudroom. "Rock?"

She was inside the birthing box. I'd never seen her there before, after the first time we put her in to get her familiar with it. I leaned against the doorway and folded my arms as I stood, studying her. She was breathing pretty heavily, but that could have been because she'd gotten so large lately with the almost full-grown pups inside her; plus, she'd just had quite a workout ripping open those presents.

"Is it time?" I whispered. Her eyes locked onto mine.

Help! they seemed to be saying, or was I imagining it?

I went to pat her head, but she growled at me and I jumped back. Yup. This was it. This was what

the vet had said would happen. It could be any-
where from one to three hours now before the
pups were actually born. What was I supposed to
do again to get ready? I was starting to panic a little.
I hoped I wouldn't get queasy.

"Just wait till Mom and Dad get home, okay,
Rocky?" I pleaded, her eyes still locked on mine
as the panting continued. "It's only a few more
hours. Like . . . four or five hours, okay? You can
hold them in." I couldn't call them to come home.
It would ruin Jake's party, and it was such a treat.
But oh, how I wished there was a grown-up in
charge right now. Tigerlily appeared in the doorway, sniffing the air. Then she turned and ran away.

I jumped up to run to the family room. "Matt!
Sam! Come quick! Rocky's having her babies!"

I stood framed in the doorway, and they both
whipped their heads to the left to look at me.

"Now?!" cried Sam.

I nodded.

"Darn! And we haven't even ordered the pizzas
yet!" said Matt, smacking his forehead.

"Dude, go order them now! Pepperoni for my
pie," said Sam.

"Order your own, fool!" said Matt, jumping up
to run into the kitchen and order his first.

Sam chased after Matt, barking orders at him.

I stood there, shaking my head from side to side. A major medical drama is about to unfold in our very own home, and all they can think about is ordering pizzas. How is this my life?

I spun on my heel and returned to the kitchen. "Could somebody please get half a plain pizza, so I can have some?"

They looked at me like *Where did you come from?* and then Matt said into the phone, "Oh, and can you also send two plain slices, please? Yes, in a box. Thanks. Bye."

"You guys are so gross. You think you're each going to eat a whole pizza by yourself?"

"I could eat two." Sam shrugged. "I don't know about you, man."

"Easily," said Matt, nodding and flexing a bicep. "These babies take work to feed."

I rolled my eyes. "Could one of you macho men please go check on the dog right now?"

They both went to the mudroom and peered in the doorway at Rocky in her bed.

"Yup. She's having some babies!" said Sam, and he left the kitchen to head back to the family room.

"Hey! Where do you think you're going?" I demanded.

He turned to me in surprise. "I'm going back to the game. Why?"

"Um, duh! The puppies?" I said sarcastically.

Sam looked incredulously at me. "There's nothing I can do. She's having her puppies. It could take hours. So just call me if you need me, like if anything goes wrong. I can drive her to the vet." And he left the room. Matt tried to follow him.

"Not so fast, mister, or I'll tell Alexis you're madly in love with her and said her name when you fell asleep in the car last week."

Matt blushed instantly. "I did not!"

I wiggled my eyebrows. "Oh yeah? Don't be so sure."

Matt sat down in a kitchen chair. "Em, there's nothing we can do for her. Look it up. She needs to deliver the babies on her own. She might bite us if we try to help her."

"Well, how are we going to know if she's in distress?" I asked.

"I don't know!"

"Oh, I wish someone was here who knew about animals!" I wailed.

"Why don't you call your boyfriend to come over?" said Matt.

"Very funny." Now it was my turn to blush.

"Anyway, Mom said no friends while they're gone."

"Then call Mrs. Barnett. She's not your friend. She can come over."

"Actually, she *is* my friend, but maybe I *will* call her."

It wasn't a bad idea. I just needed the calm voice of someone who had been through puppy births before. I needed to know there was an adult monitoring the situation.

I went to my phone and dialed her cell number. She picked up on the second ring, and I explained the situation. She was still at work and was instantly very helpful.

"Okay, I'm glad you called, especially with your parents in the city for the night. Now, don't panic. Rocky is a big, healthy girl. She's young and strong, and I highly doubt that there will be any complications. I will come over to help you, but in the meantime, could you please gather a small box, like a Rubbermaid laundry tub, and line it with newspaper and a heating pad, if you have one? Then get some old towels, and make sure the room where she's delivering is toasty—do you know how to turn up the heat? Maybe to eighty degrees? And I'll be over shortly."

"Thanks so much, Mrs. Barnett! I'm sorry to ruin your Saturday night!"

"Are you kidding? There's nothing I'd rather do on a Saturday night!" She laughed. And I believed her.

I told the boys that Mrs. Barnett was coming over, and then I scrambled around to get and do the things she had requested. Each time I checked on Rocky, she seemed to be breathing a little harder and wriggling around in her bed, like she was trying to get comfortable. She'd hardly notice me when I went in.

Mrs. Barnett arrived about half an hour after we'd spoken, right after the pizzas. She immediately washed her hands in the kitchen and then checked on Rocky. She pronounced her in excellent shape, but she did say she had one of her vets and an operating room on call in case things stalled and we needed help getting the puppies out. "But looking at her now, I think this will be rather quick," she said with a satisfied smile. She laid out a little doctor's kit with antiseptic wipes, and some scissors with rounded tips and a few other things. When I saw all that, I was happier than ever that I'd called her.

I brought a chair into the mudroom and offered Mrs. Barnett some tea, which she accepted. I set off to make it, telling the boys to go say hi and offer their help while I was in the kitchen.

By the time I got back to the mudroom, one puppy was already out! I couldn't look too closely, because I didn't want to get queasy. Mrs. Barnett said there really wasn't a lot for us to do to help Rocky, that she was a great dog and doing a fantastic job.

I sat on a chair outside the mudroom door so we could talk without me having to watch. Mrs. Barnett crooned soothing words to Rocky, encouraging her, and reported to me quietly as each pup came along.

After an hour, they were all born! Mrs. Barnett asked for an empty garbage pail and put two red medical waste bags into it, doubling them for durability. I didn't want to know what she was putting in there, but she assured me she'd take them back to ARF's garbage for proper disposal.

By the time she called us in to see, all five puppies were out and lying by Rocky's side, cleaned and feeding. Rocky was asleep, and the puppies were wriggling for position. They were tiny and had smooth pale coats, except for one, which was dark brown, and their eyes were closed. Not so cute yet, but not hideous. You could already see how they might look when they grew up.

"Are they all healthy?" asked Matt.

"Yes, they're wonderful."

"Is there a runt?" asked Sam.

I elbowed him. What a question!

"Not really. The one on the end here that keeps getting pushed out is the smallest, but not by a lot. Rocky did so well. You should be proud of her!"

"Well, she's not ours, you know. We're just dog-sitting."

"I know. Some kind of dogsitting duty you ended up with!" Mrs. Barnett laughed.

"And you!" I added. "Thank you so much, Mrs. Barnett. We could *not* have done it without you. For real."

"Oh, you would have found a way, I'm sure. Where there's a will, there's a way! And by the way," she said, looking at her watch, "you should hang a sign on the back door asking people to use the front so it doesn't get too cold in here with the door opening and closing."

"Good idea." Matt dashed off to create one on his computer, while Sam offered Mrs. Barnett a slice of reheated pizza. He hadn't finished his whole pie after all, the braggart.

She declined and headed home, and about an

hour later, in came Jake and my parents and the friends (through the front door). Jake was desperate to see Rocky and the puppies, as were his friends. We had them creep in one by one to the darkened room and peek without touching. My parents were thrilled that we'd called Mrs. Barnett, and they planned to send her flowers on Monday and make a nice donation to ARF in her honor.

"And you, Miss Em! You handled everything like a pro!" said my dad.

"We're so proud of you, sweetie," said my mom. "You're a rock."

"Rocky's a rock!" I said, and we laughed. "Now, what's Mike going to do with all those puppies?"

CHAPTER 9

Ongaro

$\mathcal{I}$ have to laugh now that I ever wondered what Mike would do with all the puppies.

Mike and Sandy rented a place in their new town that wouldn't take dogs. He told us that we could sell the puppies to recoup the costs of hosting Rocky and that he'd give Rocky to ARF to place in a new home. Well, any dummy would have known how that would turn out. I sensed Sandy was behind all of this, but I reserved my dislike for Mike for following through with it.

So on Jake's actual birthday a few days later, my parents tied a big red bow around Rocky's neck and sent her into Jake's room to wake him up. He knew what it meant immediately and spent the day telling everyone he saw about his new "baby boy puppy" (who was neither a boy nor a puppy, but whatever).

So with the new pups, plus Rocky and Tigerlily, we went from no animals to seven animals in just a few weeks. I'm not going to lie to you, our mudroom smelled gross, and the back part of the house quickly smelled like animals in general. I got used to it, but I don't think my mom will ever get over the experience. It will be better when the pups are grown and gone. We've gated in the mudroom, so now that they're up and about, they can roam freely, and they're really cute. My dad is about as into the pups as anyone could be. I find him in there all the time, just sitting and playing with them. Interestingly, Jake prefers Rocky to any of her pups, still. Tigerlily tends to them like they're her own, and Rocky doesn't seem to mind. When one of the pups goes scrambling away, Tigerlily jumps up and nudges it back toward Rocky. It's pretty cool.

"Hey, Dad, maybe we should just keep breeding Rocky! Then you could have pups around more than once!" I joked.

"Absolutely not!" he said, not even realizing I was joking.

"Okay, take it easy!" I said, backing away.

"We'll get her spayed as soon as it's medically allowed," he added.

"Okayyyy . . . ," I whispered, turning and fleeing the mudroom.

Once the dogs were a month old, we began trying to place them in earnest. Katie and her mom came, and Mrs. Brown seemed to be doing okay, but Katie reported that she'd had hives once they got home, though it might have been from Tigerlily. Katie was still working on it.

Diego brought his dad over, who was supernice. He was fine with the pups—no allergies—and they decided to bring back Diego's sister on another day, but it still hadn't happened. I know how much Diego wants one because he asks me for pics of the litter all the time and then posts them, which makes Katie anxious. Katie has her eye on the little dark brown one, which she calls Snickerdoodle, or "Snicky" for short, and she's worried someone will swoop in and adopt her before she can convince her mom. I have assured her that I will not let anything of the sort happen.

However, two "maybes" does not take any of the five pups off our hands for sure, and my parents are starting to get antsy. They hired Matt to make posters advertising the pups and to hang them around town. Mrs. Barnett has been by to visit a few times, and she took some of the posters to put up in ARF and to hand out around town. Diego has such a good track record with his Instagram account, but nothing has come up so far from his posting, even a cute photo he took of Tigerlily and Snicky, snuggled together asleep.

One Saturday morning, when the pups were six weeks old, I was delivering our weekly batch of mini cupcakes to Mona's bridal salon and showing the puppy pics to Mona and her lead sales manager, Patricia. They were oohing and aahing over the puppies' cuteness and asking all about them.

"How old do they have to be before they can leave the mom?" asked Mona.

"Eight to ten weeks is ideal," I said. I'd learned a lot about puppies lately.

"And how many have you placed?" asked Patricia.

"None," I said glumly. "I mean, don't get me wrong. I'd love to keep them all, forever, but there's just no way. . . ."

Mona was looking thoughtful. "You know, nothing personal, but these photos are just not sales photos. They're dark and too close up, and you can't really get a sense of the size of the pups. I think I have an idea. . . ."

She dashed off to her office, leaving me and Patricia to shrug at each other. Usually, Mona's ideas were good ones, so I was looking forward to hearing what she had to say.

Minutes later, she returned, clapping her hands in victory. "Okay! It is all set! Wednesday afternoon I have Ongaro here, you know my fabulous photographer from the city? He's shooting a campaign with adult models for me, and we'll have everything set up . . . lighting, backdrops, the works. Why don't you and one of those cute brothers of yours bring in the puppies, and we'll do a professional-quality pet shoot? The photos will really represent the puppies in their best light. Okay? Done! It will be divine, just divine!" she trilled.

I laughed and threw my arms around Mona. "You're the best!" I cried. "We'll do it, thank you!" I didn't know what I was in for, though.

Wednesday came, and my dad left work early to help me and Jake wrangle the pups and to drive us to the mall. We brought them in a huge carrier, and Rocky was pretty distressed, so Matt had to take her out for a walk while we piled the pups into a giant dog crate and put them in the minivan. They squealed and scratched and were generally wild and unsettled all the way there; luckily, none of them pooped in the crate.

At Mona's, the adult bridal models had just finished and were luckily back in their street clothes when we walked in, my dad and I carrying the crate between us. Ongaro the photographer was a really giant, tough guy dressed all in denim with a leather vest, but when we opened the crate and let the puppies out, he fell to his knees and started speaking baby talk to them all. It was kind of hilarious.

But that's where the good times stopped for a while and frustration took over.

The puppies were impossible to keep in one place. We'd stack them into a cute puppy pyramid, and the second we moved, they'd all slide to the floor. Or we'd line them all up, and they'd start wandering around. One of them peed; another pooped, and then his brother stepped in it. It was gross and frustrating. Even Mona was starting to wonder aloud what we'd gotten into.

Ongaro was a good sport, though. "Now you see why animal photographers get paid the big bucks!" he said in his deep voice. "It's like being a war photographer. Always on your toes, catching the action!" His camera was whirring as he took shot after shot, but there was always a pup just wandering out of the frame. Still Ongaro kept his cool. "They're just so cute! So funny! I'm falling in love!" he'd boom.

He took a break and looked at the shots with Mona. While they discussed them, I looked at my dad. "Bad idea?" I whispered.

He sighed. "Maybe not the best use of everyone's time, but they were good to do it."

A minute later, Ongaro and Mona returned. Mona clapped her hands. "Jake and Emma, in the photo please!"

"Wait, what? I look like a total slob!" I said. I was wearing dirty jeans and a flannel shirt, and my hair was in two long braids. Jake was wearing his police officer T-shirt and sweatpants.

"You look beautiful and wholesome, as always. We think you two need to be in the photo for scale. People won't realize how cute and tiny these pups are without some kind of reference."

It took a few minutes to warm Jake up to it, especially because Ongaro called for his assistant to brush Jake's hair and powder our shiny noses and foreheads, but once we sat on the drop cloth to play with the pups, we forgot about the cameras.

Ongaro clicked and whirred, and within ten minutes he said he had at least a dozen great shots, which he'd e-mail to Mona tonight when he got back to his studio.

My dad and I thanked everyone, and I gave Mona a huge hug. And just as we were leaving, Ongaro said in a resigned voice, "Okay. I'll take the dark brown one," as if we'd been begging him all afternoon.

"What?" I said, my jaw falling open in shock.

"Great!" said my dad.

"Um . . . but . . . that's the one Katie wants," I said, agonizing.

"Oh," my dad and Ongaro said at the same time.

"But is Katie really going to take her? Her mom's allergic, honey. Let's be realistic here." My dad looked at me, almost looking like one of the puppies himself.

I thought I might cry suddenly. "Um . . ." I knew he was right. I mean, what's that expression, "Don't look a gift horse in the mouth?" or "A bird in the hand is worth two in the bush"? All these animal expressions floated through my head.

Ongaro was looking at me, and then he put a warm, soft paw on my shoulder. "Listen, I will take one. I think they are adorable. I would prefer the dark one, since my signature color is choco-late brown." He gestured to his vest, his boots, and a business card he produced, all chocolate brown. "If your friend does not want it, just let me know. Otherwise, I will take one of the honey-colored ones as soon as they are ready."

"Oh, Mr. Ongaro! Thank you!" I yelped, and threw my arms around him. He patted me and laughed and said it was fine and he'd see me soon.

We crated up the pups, said our good-byes and thanks-yous, and headed out.

In the car, my dad cautioned me again. "Don't cut off your nose to spite your face," he said, and I didn't even know what that one meant. All I knew was I had to find out ASAP from Katie what her plan was.

Mona sent along ten great photos the next day, and I forwarded them to Diego and Matt for distribution. A week later, I began my campaign. I decided that the only way for people to fall in love with these dogs was to borrow them and have the chance to see them in their own homes. Specifically, Diego and Katie.

So I e-mailed them both and asked them if they'd be willing to try it.

Katie came right back to me with a yes; Diego took a day longer. But by the following weekend, they each had an eight-week-old puppy at home with them.

I checked in with them both as much as I could without seeming totally desperate. Diego posted pics all Saturday night of everyone in his family hanging around with the dog. His sister and dad looked fine to me. Katie reported that her mom was symptom free and had declared that if she was still fine by the next weekend, Snicky could stay!

By Sunday, we were fielding calls from people all around town who had seen the new Ongaro photos and wanted to come and see the pups. My parents had decided that for strangers, we'd sell the dogs for $150 each, to recoup the costs of all the food and medical bills, like for the puppies' shots and Rocky's checkups. For friends and family, the pups were free. Despite the calls, and a few visits, we didn't get any takers. I felt like Mrs. Barnett at the park with the ARF animals—lots of patters and holders but no takers.

I called Mr. Ongaro to deliver the good and bad news about the dark-brown pup, and he said it was fine because he had decided that he preferred a honey-colored one so much, he'd be changing his signature color to honey-gold

121

as soon as possible. He came by on a Tuesday night, and we gave him the pup, whom he named Scavullo after a famous fashion photographer. I thought it was a mouthful until he told me he planned to call him Lolo. Naturally, we did not charge Ongaro for the pup.

Katie called Friday, screaming with joy. Snicky was hers! I was thrilled but also so relieved that I'd stuck by my word and saved her pup for her. But then on the flip side, Diego called to say his sister had had an asthma attack, and they were likely going to have to return the pup they were calling Piper, the smallest of the litter. He was so curt on the phone that I was hurt, but then I thought of my brothers and figured it was probably because he wanted to cry and didn't want me to know. That pup came back the next day, and I gave her some extra TLC, like Diego had done for Tigerlily when I had to leave her at ARF for that extra twenty-four hours.

So that left two more pups to place, and by the end of that tenth week, we'd finally done it! A friend of my mom's—another librarian—had gotten permission from their director to bring a dog to work with her once it was housebroken, so she'd come over and selected a little pup we had called Liam, after the handsome actor Liam Carey whom we all loved. She was going to call him Melville, though, after the author. Melly. It was okay with me.

And second to last was Jinx. A young family who had seen the sign at the playground came and sat with her for hours over two days, and finally asked to take her home, turning over $150—the only money we wound up making off the pups. It was fine—it just about covered the costs, my mom said. ("About half," corrected my dad.) I think my mom was just so thrilled to get the pups placed, she would have paid people to take them at that point.

And finally, with just the one last pup of Diego's to place, we were in pretty good shape. My mom had professional cleaners come and clean the whole downstairs of the house, including throwing away the gross cardboard birthing bed. The house got back to normal (and smelling normal too), and I considered floating the idea of keeping Piper, but I knew that would be pushing my luck. Jake was just obsessed with Rocky and not as interested in the pups. Tigerlily was a wonderful addition to my life, but a little bit of work, too—feeding, brushing, playing, changing the litter box, letting her in and out. Another week passed, and the Cupcakers came to bake on Friday for Mona and for a birthday party for one of Jake's friends. We were all happy that it was almost December, and that meant a nice long break, with plenty of time for baking and playing with animals.

Jake and Rocky were snuggling on Rocky's bed when my phone rang where it was sitting on the kitchen table. I didn't recognize the number, but Rocky sat bolt upright and gave a short bark.

"Easy, girl! I got it, I got it!"

Piper came running in from the mudroom and slid on her paws the last few feet, coming to a stop just in front of me.

I answered, expecting it to be someone calling about a cupcake job.

"Hello?"

"Em?"

"Diego? Where are you calling me from?"

"The allergist's office! Cecilia just had her new allergy testing done. She's not allergic to animals at all! She's allergic to feathers and dust!"

I sat down heavily. "Wait, what? What are you saying?"

"I can have Piper! I can have the puppy!" This

time I think he actually was crying, but he didn't mind me knowing.

"DIEGO! I can't believe it!"

The Cupcakers gathered around. "What? What is it?" they asked in concern.

"Diego can have Piper! Did you hear that, girl? You're going home!" I reached down and scooped her up. "Say hi to your daddy!" I held the phone to her ear and could hear Diego babbling away in puppyspeak. She licked the phone, and I laughed and dried it on my pants, "Diego? When can you come get her?"

"We'll be there at six fifteen, right after my dad gets home. Is that okay?"

"Awesome. I am so psyched for you!"

"Me too. Thanks, Em. Thanks for keeping her for me."

"My pleasure!" I said, thanking my lucky stars that no one else had come forward in the meantime. I think I know what I would have done, but you never know when parents get crazy what they'll make you do.

I hung up the phone and looked at the Cupcakers.

"Time to make a batch o' pupcakes!" I cried. "And tint the frosting honey-gold!"

"Yippee!" they cried.

"Did you hear that, Rocky? Your daughter's going to live with Emma's boyfriend!" said Jake, over on the dog bed.

"Awwww! He's so cute!" squealed Mia.

I rolled my eyes at Jake. But I couldn't stop smiling.

Want another sweet cupcake?
Here's a sneak peek
of the next book in the

CUPCAKE DIARIES

series:

Alexis
cupcake
crush

Health Cakes

I took a big bite of a chocolate cupcake. "Mmm! Yummy! Vitamins and minerals!" I mumbled through the crumbs. But it was *not* yummy. Not yummy at *all*. "Ugh. These are horrible!" I yelled and ran to the garbage to spit out my bite. "Sorry, Katie," I added sheepishly.

Emma and Mia laughed, and Katie shook her head, but she was smiling.

The Cupcake Club was helping me out— *again!*—with a project, but for once it was something we were all experts in: cupcakes! This time, it was my project for the science fair, and I had decided to prove that cupcakes are good for you. I know, it sounds crazy—like yet another marketing scheme of mine—but it turns out it's true. Under certain circumstances, anyway. You needed the right ingredients.

So, according to my research, chocolate is good for you; especially dark chocolate. It is good for your blood and liver and cholesterol, and when you eat it, it releases endorphins, which relax you and make you feel happy. So, dark chocolate cupcakes with dark chocolate frosting are a must for the science fair. It's just a teeeeeny bit difficult to make dark chocolate taste really good without adding lots of sugar (the bad thing about sugar is that it cancels out a lot of the healthy things about dark chocolate). That's why improving sugarless taste is one thing we were working on in our "test kitchen," which was at Emma's house today.

Another way cupcakes can be good for you is if you swap out unhealthy ingredients for healthier ones. Like, instead of oil or butter, you can use applesauce, and instead of sugar, you can swap in either a sugar substitute, like stevia, or something naturally sweet, like sweet potatoes. Katie's really good at that kind of thing, because she just intuitively understands the principles of baking. My mom would be too, if she were a baker, 'cause she's really into healthy eating. But for her, healthy eating *excludes* cupcakes, and I think that is very, very sad. (And so does my dad, who *loves* cupcakes!)

If we can reduce the sugar and fat in our basic cupcake and frosting recipes, and up the dark chocolate and then add fruit or veggies, then we can have a healthy recipe I can use for the science fair (not to mention samples I can hand out to the judges!). It's just been really slow going, and honestly, it's starting to seem like we'll never get them to taste good.

Mia's convinced if we make them look pretty enough, people will just eat them and not care, but I disagree, and so does Emma.

"It's not about looks!" said Emma.

"Easy for you to say," I teased. Emma's a model, and you know how really pretty people can sometimes take their looks for granted and, like, not notice them? She's like that. I suppose it's a good quality, but it can be kind of annoying, anyway.

Emma rolled her eyes. "You know what I mean."

Mia nodded. "I disagree. They have to be visually appealing."

"Mia's right," said Katie, her brow furrowed in concentration. "A lot of our perception is visual, even when it comes to taste. A good appearance makes us imagine one thing while a bad appearance makes us imagine something else. Same with the aroma. If they smell good, that's half the battle.

You should make all that a part of your research, too."

I sat on a stool in Emma's kitchen. "Well, we definitely don't want people imagining . . ." I lifted a jar Katie had emptied into the new batter, and read the label. "Sweet potato puree? Yuck!"

"You'd be surprised," Katie said wisely.

I sighed. "That's why we pay you the big bucks, Katie. You're the taste doctor." I shrugged and pulled over the notebook I was using to keep track of the recipes to see what Katie had written in it. What I saw there was much more to my liking: quantities, measurements, pricing, calorie counts . . . in a word, numbers! My favorite thing.

"Six ninety-nine for one little can of sweet potatoes?" I asked incredulously.

"They're organic, and they're pricey when they're processed like that. You could bake and scoop your own. It would be a lot cheaper, but they might not be as smooth as the professionally pureed ones," said Katie.

I pushed the jar away. "Well, let's just see how they taste. Maybe they're worth it, and we'll scrimp on something else."

The phone rang, and Emma went to answer it. She took a message and rejoined us.

"I've heard of people even using baby food," said Emma.

"Eww! In baked goods?" I asked.

"Uh-huh," Emma said, giggling. She picked up a yucky cupcake and tried to feed it to me, like I was a baby. "Open up, Lexi . . . ," she said in baby talk.

I clamped my mouth shut and shook my head.

"Come on! Yummy, yummy!" she joked, wiggling the cupcake toward my mouth, like she was feeding a toddler.

I closed my eyes and shook my head harder, and she grabbed my chin to try to force open my mouth. Then I started laughing, and we were wrestling, and I fell off the stool. Right then, Emma's brother Matt, the crush of my life, strolled in from practice.

He looked at me on the floor and then at Emma trying to shove the cupcake at me, and he shook his head, but he was laughing. "If only people knew what went on behind the closed doors of the Cupcake Club. I could sell a magazine article about it for a fortune!"

"Please, don't!" I cried, jumping to my feet.

"How much is my silence worth?" he joked.

I waved my arm at the dozen healthy (and awful)

cupcakes on the counter. "These are all yours!" I said generously.

Matt's eyes lit up. "Seriously?"

I shared a smile with the other Cupcakers. "Uh-huh!"

Then he looked at me skeptically. "What's the catch?" He narrowed his eyes and lifted a cupcake to inspect it.

"Why would there be a catch?" I asked innocently.

Matt looked at the cupcake suspiciously. He turned it all around. It was small and dense, and the dark chocolate frosting was thick and glossy. It looked delicious. Next, Matt lifted it to his nose and gave it a whiff.

Katie nudged me. "See? Looks and smell count."

"Hmm. Good observation," I agreed.

We all stood with bated breath as Matt took a tentative nibble. He looked at us looking at him, and his brow furrowed. "It's . . ." He was about to say "good," but then the lack of sugar hit him.

He spun and hurried to the garbage and spat his cupcake on top of mine.

"*Blech!* Who forgot the sugar?!" he cried.

We all giggled. "They're healthy cupcakes. They're good for you!" I chirped.

"Yeah, because you try one bite and then you don't eat the rest. That's why it's good for you," Matt retorted, scowling. He wagged his finger at me as I laughed. "You owe me, missy!"

"They're my project for the science fair. You're our guinea pig," I admitted.

Matt got a funny look on his face. "The science fair? Already? Oh. That's cool. Who are you partners with?"

"Partners? Who gets partners for a science fair?" I laughed, still giddy. "I'm my own partner. Plus my silent partners, the Cupcake Club!"

Mia waved and I laughed again.

"Oh. Well, that should be a winner," said Matt, but he didn't sound superenthusiastic. He hoisted his backpack onto his shoulder and turned to go up to his room.

"Sam Perry called," Emma said as he retreated.

"Who?" Matt turned back around.

"Sam Perry?" said Emma.

"Who's Sam Perry?" I asked.

Emma shrugged.

Matt had a funny look on his face that I couldn't read. "New at school," he said, and he wandered off.

"Who's Sam Perry?" I repeated to Emma when Matt was out of earshot.

"I have no idea," she said, looking down at her nails.

"Weird. Never heard of him," I said. I wondered briefly why Matt had acted so odd. But maybe I was just imagining things.

Emma glanced at me like she was going to say something, but then she seemed to change her mind and instead said, "Katie, what about applesauce?"

Katie nodded. "We can try that. It's always the first suggestion. It's just that applesauce does have a lot of sugar in it itself. You kind of might as well use real sugar."

Katie made a third batter now, opening the jar of applesauce and measuring out the proper amount. I like applesauce (much more than sweet potatoes), so I had high hopes for this batch.

Meanwhile, we needed to start brainstorming about our real work, the kind that earns money. My favorite kind!

I opened the ledger where we keep track of all our business and scanned the recent entries. "Oh, we've got a sweet sixteen coming up," I said. "In two weekends."

"Cool. That could be fun. Just for starters, I'm thinking all pink and ruffly, like a *quinceañera*," said

Mia, referencing the Latina rite of passage she was looking forward to in her own life.

"Whose party is it?" asked Katie.

"Um, Martine Donay?" I wasn't sure I was pronouncing the name right. I'd never heard of her.

"Martine Donay?!" said Mia incredulously. "She's having a sweet sixteen? With *cupcakes*?"

Katie and I exchanged a worried glance. "Um, yeah?" I said.

Mia laughed and smacked the counter with her palm. "Wow. I've seen it all now. Who'd a-thunk it? Martine Donay!"

"Who *is* this person?" I asked. I was getting a little annoyed. "Emma, do you know her?"

Emma smiled. "Yup. She's not exactly the sweet sixteen–type. She lives around the corner. I see her sometimes, but I don't think she would know me."

"She's a friend of Dan's, for starters," said Mia, referring to her stepbrother, who's a heavy-metal music nut.

"Oh," I said. That told me a lot.

"A total rocker chick," continued Mia. "Black leather, ripped jeans, chains—the works. I can't imagine what kind of cupcakes she'd want."

"Well, it was her mother who contacted us," I said, looking at my notes.

"We'll need to get in touch with them and see what they're hoping for," said Emma. "This ought to be interesting."

I made a note in the ledger and agreed to contact Mrs. Donay and set up a meeting.

"Anything else lined up for that weekend?" asked Katie.

"Two kids' birthday parties—a seven-year-old boy, Sawyer Reese, and a five-year-old girl, Libby Murray—and this weekend, only Mona's minis, as usual, and book club for Mrs. Gormley. She requested the bacon caramel cupcakes. I think it's that same book club we've baked for in the past; it just moves around from house to house. They love our bacon cupcakes."

"Best idea I ever had!" crowed Emma as she helped Katie ladle the two revised batches of batter into the cupcake liners in the muffin pan. "And you all laughed at me!"

"Live and learn, that's one of my mottoes," I said with a shrug.

"Oh, Alexis, what *isn't* one of your mottoes?" teased Mia.

"It does help to have organizing principles, you know," I said with a sniff, but I was really only pretending to be annoyed. I know my friends love me and all my quirkiness. That's why the Cupcake Club is so much fun. I get to totally relax and be my true self with these three girls.

"Yes, you're very organized," agreed Katie with a gentle teasing smile. "So, what are we doing for the kids' birthdays?"

I looked back at my notes again. "Okay, they each only need two dozen. Sawyer is having a dinosaur-themed party with a dig for 'fossils,' so he wants something that looks like mud. Libby wants pink ballet-themed cupcakes with fluffy pink frosting."

"Cute!" said Mia. We all nodded.

"Any other cupcake business?" asked Emma.

I glanced around the ledger page. "Well, we were talking about getting a quote from Matt for some new flyers to hand out to new clients."

"Ooh, good idea!" agreed Mia. "He does such a nice job," she said to Emma. "My mom recommended him to her boss for their next graphic design needs."

"Cool! Thanks! I'll tell him," said Emma.

Matt is very talented at graphic design and computer stuff. We've used him for posters and flyers and mailings and more, and we've always been really impressed by his talent. I especially like using him for projects 'cause then I get to hang out with him more and it gives me an excuse to call or text or e-mail him!

"I'll send him an e-mail for a quote." I made a note to myself. "We should brainstorm about what we're looking to say about ourselves and what we offer."

It's pretty cool how far we've come as a business from when we first started, and I'm not saying that to brag just 'cause I'm the CEO. I like thinking about things like mission statements and profit-and-loss sheets; these are the things I work on in the Future Business Leaders of America, a club at school, and they always come in handy in real life.

"Just do a quick thing at the top, like, 'Four stylish friends plus professional baking experience times good taste equals the Cupcake Club,'" suggested Mia.

"That is awesome!" I replied, writing as fast as I could to get it all down. I love math, so any math-themed thing is up my alley.

Katie looked thoughtful. "Or you could do a recipe, like 'two cups experience, one cup great taste, one cup style . . .' uh . . ."

Mia warmed to Katie's idea and kept it going. "'Four tablespoons friendship . . .'"

"'A splash of zest'!" added Emma.

"'Makes: one great party treat'!" I added.

"That's so good. I love it," Mia said, grinning.

"What about your equation idea, though? I loved that too," I said.

Mia shook her head. "No, save that for something else. I mean, write it in the ledger and we'll use it later."

"Okay. This is great. Thanks!"

"How much longer on these cupcakes?" asked Mia.

Katie looked at the timer. "Nine minutes."

"I hope these work!" I said nervously. "No offense," I added.

"None taken," said Katie. "I hope they work too. Anyway, it could be good for us to offer a healthy option in cupcakes, too."

I smacked my head. "Of course! Maybe if we hit on the right thing, we can put that in our flyer too. Like, 'Now introducing our line of healthy options . . .'"

We cleaned up and chatted, and soon the cupcakes were out of the oven and frosted. Katie arranged them on two plates, and we all sampled one of each.

I tried the applesauce first, cautiously this time.

The texture was good; they were nice and moist. I rolled the bite around in my mouth and found it pleasantly sweet—not overly so, like a regular cupcake, but pretty darn good!

"Hey! The applesauce ones are pretty good!" I said in surprise.

Mia was wide-eyed. She swallowed. "The sweet potato ones are *really* good!"

I made a face—ew, sweet potato puree—but I reached for one and then popped a bite into my mouth. She was right!

"Oh, Katie!" I said through my mouthful of cake. "*These* are delicious!"

Katie was chewing thoughtfully. "Thanks," she said. "I think the sweet potato ones are actually the better ones." She swallowed. "But do they have kind of a funny aftertaste?"

I moved my tongue around in my mouth. "I don't know. Maybe. Not bad, though."

"I think they're great," said Emma. "Do you want me to call in the experts?"

Any chance to see Matt! "Sure!" I agreed.

"They're not that picky, remember," warned Emma. "Hey, boys!" she yelled.

Soon, Emma's brothers—Jake, Matt, and Sam—were thundering into the kitchen, and the cupcakes were quickly depleted. They resoundingly voted for the sweet potato version, and Katie decided to reuse the applesauce concept as a new healthy apple-cinnamon recipe for the fall.

"Are these really good for us?" Jake asked incredulously.

I nodded solemnly. "Packed with veggies. Can you tell?"

Jake shook his head. "You're tricking me!"

I looked at my friends. "That's just the reaction we were hoping for!" and we all high-fived.

Want more

cupcakeDiaries?

Visit **CupcakeDiariesBooks.com**
for the series trailer, excerpts, activities,
and everything you need for throwing
your own cupcake party!

Still Hungry?
There's always room for

another Cupcake!

Katie and the cupcake cure

CUPCAKE DIARIES

by Coco Simon

Mia in the mix

CUPCAKE DIARIES

by Coco Simon

Emma on thin icing

CUPCAKE DIARIES

by Coco Simon

Alexis and the perfect recipe

CUPCAKE DIARIES

by Coco Simon

Katie, batter up!

CUPCAKE DIARIES

by Coco Simon

Mia's baker's dozen

CUPCAKE DIARIES

Emma all stirred up!

CUPCAKE DIARIES

by Coco Simon

Alexis cool as a cupcake

CUPCAKE DIARIES

by Coco Simon

Katie and the cupcake war

CUPCAKE DIARIES

Mia's boiling point

CUPCAKE DIARIES

Emma, smile and say "cupcake"

CUPCAKE DIARIES

Alexis gets frosted

CUPCAKE DIARIES

by Coco Simon

CUPCAKE DIARIES — Katie's new recipe

CUPCAKE DIARIES — Mia a matter of taste

CUPCAKE DIARIES — Emma sugar and spice and everything nice

CUPCAKE DIARIES — Alexis and the missing ingredient

CUPCAKE DIARIES — Katie sprinkles and surprises

CUPCAKE DIARIES — Mia fashion plates and cupcakes

CUPCAKE DIARIES — Emma lights! camera! cupcakes!

CUPCAKE DIARIES — Alexis the icing on the cupcake

CUPCAKE DIARIES — Katie starting from scratch

CUPCAKE DIARIES — Mia's recipe for disaster

CUPCAKE DIARIES — Emma's not-so-sweet dilemma

CUPCAKE DIARIES — Alexis's cupcake cupid

CUPCAKE DIARIES — Katie sprinkled secrets

CUPCAKE DIARIES — Mia the way the cupcake crumbles

CUPCAKE DIARIES — Emma raining cats and dogs . . . and cupcakes!

CUPCAKE DIARIES — Alexis cupcake crush

If you liked

CUPCAKE  DIARIES

be sure to check out these

other series from

Simon Spotlight

If you like reading about the adventures of Katie, Mia, Emma, and Alexis, you'll love Alex and Ava, stars of the It Takes Two series!

sew Zoey

Zoey's clothing design blog puts her on the A-list in the fashion world . . . but when it comes to school, will she be teased, or will she be a trendsetter? Find out in the Sew Zoey series:

SewZoeyBooks.com • Published by Simon Spotlight • Kids.SimonandSchuster.com

You're invited to MORE

CREEPOVERS!

HAVE YOU BEEN TO EVERY ONE?

Did you LOVE reading this book?

Visit the Whyville...

IN THE MIDDLE BOOK HIVE

Where you can:

- Discover great books!
- Meet new friends!
- Read exclusive sneak peeks and more!

Log on to visit now!
bookhive.whyville.net

Looking for another great book?
Find it
IN THE MIDDLE.

Fun, fantastic books for kids
in the in-be**TWEEN** age.

IntheMiddleBooks.com

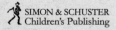

Coco Simon always dreamed of opening a cupcake bakery but was afraid she would eat all of the profits. When she's not daydreaming about cupcakes, Coco edits children's books and has written close to one hundred books for children, tweens, and young adults, which is a lot less than the number of cupcakes she's eaten. Cupcake Diaries is the first time Coco has mixed her love of cupcakes with writing.